BY JAMIE EDMUNDSON

ME THREE
Og-Grim-Dog: The Three-Headed Ogre
Og-Grim-Dog and The Dark Lord
Og-Grim-Dog and The War of The Dead
Og-Grim-Dog: Ogre's End Game

THE WEAPON TAKERS SAGA
TORIC'S DAGGER
BOLIVAR'S SWORD
THE JALAKH BOW
THE GIANTS' SPEAR

Og-Grim-Dog and the Dark Lord

JAMIE EDMUNDSON

Og-Grim-Dog and the Dark Lord
Book 2 of Me Three
Copyright © 2020 by Jamie Edmundson.
All rights reserved.
First Edition: 2020

Rarn
Publishing

ISBN 978-1-912221-07-3

Author website jamieedmundson.com

Cover Artwork: Andrey Vasilchenko

For Ben

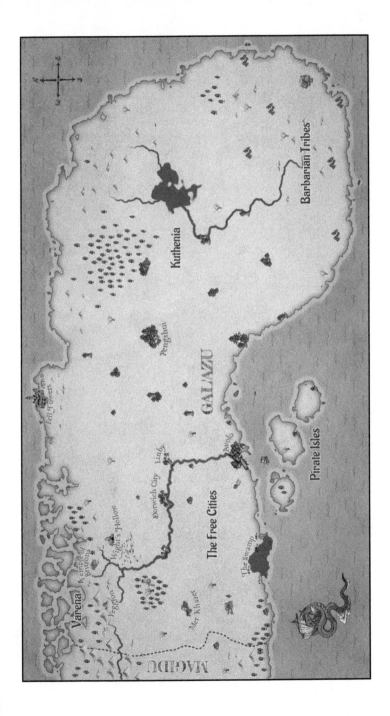

A DARK TALE

It was the second night at the Flayed Testicles. And it was story time.

Not very much had changed since the night before. There was the Landlord, at the bar, preparing himself for tonight's instalment. In between pulling pints and serving food, he could be heard doing vocal exercises, ensuring his voice was in good condition for the performance.

Close by sat the Recorder at his table. He wore the same clothes, in the same poor condition, as yesterday. It seemed that any money the Recorder earned (and let's be honest, humble writers make ever so little), he had spent on the tools of his trade. A fresh pile of parchment sat waiting to be written on, and his quill rested in a bottle of ink.

The same old regulars of the Testicles were in attendance, seated in their usual places. But more customers had come tonight. Word had spread around town about last night's revelations and no-one wanted to miss out on the sequel. Even some out-of-towners had arrived, from the nearby farmsteads and hamlets. In the quiet and peaceable backwater that was Magidu, tonight's storytelling was box office.

Finally, everyone settled down and a hush descended on the inn. All attention was on the ogre standing at the bar and the figure at the table in front of him, quill now in hand, ready to adorn his pages with inky black text.

'It is a dark tale we have come to tell tonight,' intoned the ogre's first head. The customers of the Testicles looked at one another with excitement, more than one commenting that they had goosebumps. There was something intensely satisfying about dark tales told late at night.

'Interesting,' commented the Recorder.

The ogre's eyes narrowed suspiciously at the comment.

'*Why* is that interesting?'

'Well, it's just that the last story ended on a positive note. You had decided to leave the safety of your cavern in Darkspike Dungeon and strike out, looking for adventure.'

'Yes,' agreed the second head, slightly appeased. 'But remember also, we had tried to become heroes and weren't accepted. The Bureau of Dungeoneering banned ogres from adventuring and ordered us to leave Mer Khazer. Is it any wonder that we took a darker path?'

'I suppose not,' conceded the Recorder. 'But that wasn't your intention when you left your dungeon? I'm just trying to get your motivation right.'

The ogre shrugged. 'Good intentions are one thing. Habits are another. Two steps forward and one step back. Do you think because we decided to change our ways, stop hiding from the world and embrace it, that it simply just happened? Life is never so easy, is it?'

'Oh, that's good,' said the Recorder, enthused. 'Let me just write that down,' he added, and his quill scratched along the parchment. 'You know, I really think that's something we could improve on from last night's story. No offence intended. Just make the whole thing a bit more original, and really try to say something, you know?'

'I was saying the exact same thing before, wasn't I?' said the third head, looking across at his brothers. They said nothing in reply, but each looked a little glum. 'This time, originality and creativity are the buzzwords. If this story comes across as corny, cheap imitation; or pastiche in any way—I really want you to say so. That goes for you lot as well,' he added, addressing the rest of the Testicles. 'We won't be offended in the slightest. The last thing we want is for this to sound like some kind of lazy parody or rip-off.'

STUCK IN THE MUD

What are you doing in my swamp?' Dog shouted at the goblin.

Grim sighed. It was very rude. And anyway, why was it Dog's swamp? He was always so possessive.

'I've come to deliver a letter,' said the goblin, fishing it out of the sack that hung around his shoulder.

'Wait a minute,' said Grim. 'It's Gary, isn't it?'

The goblin grinned, pleased that Grim remembered him.

'Yes. I've been branching out into the delivery service. 'Goblin Post: we go where others fear to tread.' It's becoming quite lucrative.'

'How wonderful,' said Dog sarcastically.

'Og!' Grim said to Og, his other brother. 'Look who's here, with a letter.'

Og woke with a snort. 'What? Who?'

'It's Gary, from Darkspike Dungeon.'

Og's eyes slowly focused on the goblin. He frowned. 'I don't recall a Gary from Darkspike Dungeon.'

Grim sighed. 'Well, just read the letter, will you?'

Og took the letter from the goblin and gave him a coin.

'Good luck with the business, Gary,' Grim offered.

'Thanks. Good luck with the...swamp,' said Gary, before heading back the way he had come.

Grim walked off in the opposite direction, deeper into the swamp. In a clearing, underneath the stump of a long dead giant mallorn tree, was the home they had made. Grim got to his knees and his brothers helped him to crawl underneath into their house. Once they were seated by their window, Og and Dog took the letter from its envelope, and Og began to read.

WRITTEN AT THE BRUISED BOLLOCKS

DEAR OG-GRIM-DOG,

I HOPE YOU ARE ENJOYING YOUR NEW HOME.

THINGS ARE NO DIFFERENT HERE. AMID THE ADVENTURING, THE POLITICAL GAMES CONTINUE. I FEAR THAT DIRECTOR BARCLAY IS PLANNING A MOVE AGAINST ELVES AND HALFLINGS NEXT. SANDON AND I ARE TRYING TO ORGANISE AN OPPOSITION, BUT SOME ADVENTURERS SEEM TO THINK THEY WILL BENEFIT FROM OUR EXPULSION.

I HAVE HEARD NOTHING MORE OF GURIN FUCKAXE. I WOULD LOVE TO COME AND VISIT YOU SOME TIME, WHEN THINGS HAVE CALMED DOWN. HOWEVER, SOMEONE WAS ASKING AFTER YOU, AND TOLD ME THEY INTENDED ON PAYING YOU A CALL! BROTHER KANE! DO LOOK OUT FOR HIM, HE MAY NOT BE AS COMPETENT AT NAVIGATING A SWAMP AS YOU ARE.

WELL, THAT'S IT FROM ME FOR NOW,

LOVE RAYA

Grim sighed. No-one spoke for a while.

'How did we end up here?' asked Og at last.

They had wandered aimlessly around Gal'azu for weeks. They had not been able to decide on a goal and had found nowhere hospitable enough to settle. They had found some peace in the swamp, but that was only because it was so wretched here that no-one else wanted it.

'Because there's no place in this world for a three-headed ogre,' answered Dog bitterly. 'In the civilized lands, the humans want to kill us; in the wilds, the trolls want to kill us. We were kicked out of the Bureau of Dungeoneering. Maybe we should just go back to our cavern.'

'Oh no, please,' said Grim. 'Give it a bit more time.'

'There's no time for us,' continued Dog morosely. 'There's no place for us.'

'Going back there would be like giving up on life,' Grim argued. 'Something will turn up. Raya said Brother Kane is coming to visit

6

us. Let's at least wait here until then. You never know, he might be able to help us.'

Dog gave him a sceptical look. 'You're a fool if you trust that one. He's hiding something. I can smell it on him.'

'Don't be silly, Dog,' said Grim, trying not to get irritated with him.

'Quiet a second,' said Og. 'I thought I heard something.'

Og-Grim-Dog stayed silent, three pairs of ears listening to the sounds of the swamp.

'Is that…singing?' Grim asked at last.

'Sounds like it,' Dog agreed.

'Maybe Brother Kane has arrived?' Og suggested. 'It probably wouldn't take him much longer to walk here as it does for the goblins to deliver Raya's letter.'

'Have you ever known Brother Kane to sing?' Grim asked him. 'Come on, let's investigate.'

The ogre crawled back out of their house and began to search for the origin of the singing. Sound could carry strangely in the swamp and it took them a good while to locate the direction it came from. But in the end Grim found himself trudging through a cypress wood, the singing getting louder as he did so. He had got used to wading through water in the last few weeks. His feet weren't in great shape: the wet and mud had taken their toll and he now insisted that Og and Dog carefully dry them every time they returned to their house, to keep away infection.

'There,' said Dog, pointing.

Ahead, following a winding path across a patch of land that poked out of the water, was an animal. To be precise, a donkey. It was singing a cheerful tune. Singing it very badly.

'Well,' said Og after a while. 'Have you ever heard of a magical talking donkey before?'

'Can't say that I have,' said Dog. 'Come on, Grim. Let's catch up to the little fellow.'

Back at their house under the tree stump, Og-Grim-Dog felt a little better about life. A warm fire and a hot meal can cheer most people up, ogres included.

'Here ya go, Grim,' Dog said, offering him a spitted chunk of chargrilled meat. 'Donkeys are usually quite tough, but that little fellow turned out to be very tasty. Must be the magical talking part of him that adds the flavour.'

A WAY OUT

Brother Kane arrived in the swamp the next day. There was enough donkey left over to offer him lunch, but the cleric repeatedly explained that he had brought his own provisions with him.

They sat down to eat and after a while Brother Kane gave Og-Grim-Dog one of his beatific smiles.

'I didn't come here solely as a social call,' the cleric explained.

'Oh yeah?' asked Og, his mouth still full.

'I heard about your situation and I couldn't help thinking that I could offer you a solution to it.'

'Well, we're all ears to any thoughts you may have,' said Grim. 'Truth is, we've got ourselves stuck in a bit of a rut here. Finding it hard to find a path out.'

'Yes,' agreed Brother Kane. 'Now, what I'm about to tell you is between you and me and must stay that way. If you feel unable to keep what I say in confidence, then I will simply stop right here and now, say no more of it, and no offence taken.'

The brothers shared a look. 'We can keep a secret, Brother Kane,' Og said, speaking for them. 'Don't worry about that.'

'Excellent. Now, this may come as a bit of a shock. I haven't been honest, either with you or anyone else in Mer Khazer. The truth is, I am evil. I am under orders to infiltrate the dungeoneering community in Mer Khazer, while posing as a goodly priest.'

'I knew it!' cried Dog excitedly. 'What did I tell you?' he crowed.

'Well,' said Grim. 'Dog did guess as much, but you certainly fooled me and Og and everyone else. So, your visits to the orphanage; the old people's home?'

'Part of my cover. I don't really like children very much.'

'I see. And whose orders do you follow?'

'Well, this is the point. I work for the Dark Lord, as one of his henchmen. He aims to spread his influence across Gal'azu. And so, to my solution. You, Og-Grim-Dog, would make an excellent henchman. I'm sure a three-headed ogre is just the kind of character that the Dark Lord would welcome with open arms. And precious few others have been welcoming to you. My suggestion is that you travel to the Dark Lord's stronghold and ask to serve him. I can't promise anything with complete certainty, but I am sure that if you explain that I sent you, you will be found a place in his service. Here, I have a map that has his secret location on it.'

The cleric pulled a piece of parchment from his travelling sack and offered it. Dog took it without hesitation.

'I know you will want to think about the idea and discuss it amongst yourselves. Well,' he added, getting to his feet, 'if I leave now, I can return to the town before the sun sets. Good luck, whatever you decide to do. Here, let me give you a blessing.'

Og-Grim-Dog allowed the priest to flick his vial of water into their faces, and then he was gone.

'Well,' said Grim, feeling the need to say something, though he wasn't sure what.

'I'm not happy about turning to the dark side,' Og stated.

'What other options do we have?' asked Dog, studying the map that Brother Kane had given them. 'Here's the stronghold,' he said, jabbing a thick finger at the map. 'The least we can do is go and find out what he might offer us.'

Grim could feel an argument brewing. As usual, he would find himself in the middle of it and have the deciding vote. But this time, he already knew which way he was going to lean. They needed to get out of this swamp, and Brother Kane's proposition was the only one they had.

✻

Og-Grim-Dog left the swamp behind them. Grim was pleased that his feet would now be spared further wading through the damp bog. But instead, his legs had to carry them a long way, to the other end of Gal'azu.

When they travelled in the Great Outside, Og and Dog covered their heads, so that they drew as little attention to themselves as possible. Grim had to be careful about the routes to take. They would be treated with hostility virtually everywhere they went, and they really didn't want to be diverted into a conflict or chased from one place to the next. So, they moved cross-country, avoiding settlements and well-used paths; when they stopped, they would take turns at keeping watch, moving on if they were the slightest bit concerned that they had been observed.

The closer they came to their destination, the more remote and wild the land about them became. It was barren and rocky, and Grim increasingly found it hard going. In the end, he decided to take a road that seemed to lead them in exactly the right direction.

'Why is this Dark Lord's stronghold located as far from anywhere else as possible?' Dog grumbled from inside his sack on the fourth day. 'What's the sense in that?'

'Perhaps he's thinking about safety?' Grim suggested. Honestly, he didn't really care much about what the reasons might be, but since Og was fast asleep on his other side, he felt obliged to answer his brother's question. After all, Dog carried the map, and it would be a right pain if he fell into one of his moods.

'You'd have thought,' Dog responded, 'that if you were intent on taking over the world, you'd start off in a more convenient location.'

'Mmm,' Grim agreed. At this point he was just hoping that the stronghold would come into view. He was tired and their supplies had dwindled down to nothing.

'I assure you,' came a voice, 'the Dark Lord doesn't need to worry about his safety. He has the most loyal servants working for him.'

From behind a boulder, to the side of the road, a figure appeared. At first sight, it reminded Grim of Raya Sunshine, though this was clearly a male figure. But he had a totally different colouring to Og-Grim-Dog's elven friend. His skin colour was similar to the ogre's—if anything, a darker shade of grey; while his long hair, that blew in the wind, was white as snow.

'Who are you?' Dog asked him as he removed the sack from his head, blinking at the figure.

'My name is Wro'Kuburni'-Dy-Hrath'Simbowa. But you can call me Wro'Kuburni'-Dy-Hrath.'

Dog made a face. 'We'll call you Simba thank you very much. What do you want?'

'I am a dark elf, and a servant of—'

'An elf?'

'No, not an elf. A dark elf. Very different. My people live—'

Dog puffed out a breath. 'You're an elf. The Bull Ogres of the Plains and the Ridged Back Ogres of the Mountains just call themselves ogres. Don't get pretentious about it.'

Wro'Kuburni'-Dy-Hrath'Simbowa frowned. 'I must admit I wasn't aware of the difference between those types of ogres, but I assure you, my people are very different from our elven cousins. For a start, we are much more on board with the whole evil thing than they are. Hence, I serve the Dark Lord.'

'Oh good,' said Grim, trying to wrestle the conversation towards something productive. 'We are on our way to see him, as a matter of fact. Maybe you would be able to take us to his stronghold?'

The dark elf smiled. 'I guessed as much. This road only leads to Fell Towers. The only people who walk it are those who serve the Dark Lord, those who wish to serve him, or those who have come to do him harm. I thought you might fall into the second category?'

'That's right,' said Grim. Then, feeling that more needed to be said, added 'We've come for the job of henchman.'

'Ah,' said the dark elf. 'Well, that's my job as it happens. Come, I will accompany you on the last part of your journey and introduce you to the right person when we get there.'

FELL TOWERS

Fell Towers, stronghold of the Dark Lord, was built on a crag at the edge of the world. Beyond it, waves lashed at the rocks below. The stronghold itself had been constructed with black granite. The thick, compact walls at the base of the building gave way to several thin towers at the top, that reached into the sky like skeletal fingers. In all their travels, Grim didn't think he had ever seen a single building that covered so much space.

The road they had followed ended at a massive pair of tall, black gates. To Grim's eyes, the gates were too large to be practical for defence and suggested that their owner was more concerned with appearance.

'We're here,' said Grim, leaning over to Og.

With a groan, Og took the sack from his head. 'Thank Lord—who in Fiery Gehenna is that?' he added, gesturing towards the dark elf.

'My name is Wro'Kuburni'-Dy-Hrath'Simbowa. But your brothers have decided to call me Simba.'

'Hmm,' said Og suspiciously. 'You look like a dark elf to me.'

'I am.'

'I thought dark elves were evil.'

'We are.'

'Oh yeah, right. I forgot we were doing the whole evil thing,' Og said with a sigh. Reluctantly, he offered his hand, and the dark elf took it.

Simba then marched over to the gates and kicked at them with his thick boots until a helmeted figure appeared above them. 'Password?' it shouted down.

'Nefarious,' Simba shouted up.

'That was last week's password.'

'I've been away on the Dark Lord's business for days,' Simba responded. 'I've just got back.'

'Oh. Alright then. Give us a moment.'

The ogre and the dark elf waited beneath the stronghold until one of the gates began to move, creaking open. Once it had opened sufficiently wide enough, they strode through. Og-Grim-Dog found themselves in a courtyard open to the elements. At various points along the external walls, stone steps led up to the battlements, where the ogre could see more figures like the one Simba had spoken to. They all looked the same: helmeted, with a black and silver uniform over metal armour.

Four more guarded the entrance into the stronghold's main keep. If the main gates and the thin towers were partly for show, this squat building was a different kind of affair. It looked like it was well capable of holding off a determined assault. Although, Grim mused, why an army would traipse all the way here wasn't clear.

Simba gestured over to the keep and led Og-Grim-Dog towards its tunnelled entrance. He approached the four guards without a word and as he did so, he rapped his knuckles on one of the helmets.

'Menials,' he commented as he strode into the keep.

'Menials?' Grim asked, following behind.

'They are the minions of the Dark Lord. They serve as guards and common soldiers in his legions. The role of henchman is much more high status. If you can offer the right kind of skillset you could end up as a henchman. If not, it's a life as a menial for you. Come, I'll take you straight to the person who will make that decision.'

'The Dark Lord?' asked Dog, sounding excited.

Simba made a face, though Grim couldn't interpret what it meant. Dark elves, he decided, had a different set of expressions to humans.

'No,' said Simba. 'His adviser, Lilith. She has a big say on operational decisions.'

They were standing in a tall hallway, decorated in deep reds and creams, with elaborate candelabra along its walls that shed light on the paintings and tapestries that hung there. Grim could smell the kitchens—almost taste the dinner that wafted on the air. He heard the clink of crockery coming from the refectory. His stomach rumbled with hunger. But he made himself ignore it all and follow Simba to a set of wide stairs that curved their way up to the next floor.

More menials guarded the stairs.

'I've come to see Mistress Lilith,' Simba announced to them.

'Who's that?' asked one of the helmeted figures, gesturing at Og-Grim-Dog.

'A new henchman. Possibly.'

'Oh. I believe Mistress Lilith is in her rooms.'

The guards stood aside and let them climb the stairs.

'We are about to enter the nexus of the Dark Lord's empire,' Simba explained as they ascended to the next floor of the fortress. 'Not everyone is allowed up here.'

The stairs opened on a landing, from where Grim could look down the twisting staircase and all the way to the hallway below. Simba led them to one of the landing exits and into an open plan office. Here, officials sat at desks surrounded by piles of paper, books, maps and all the other paraphernalia of reading and writing. Some worked in silence, while others whispered in small groups. The room had an atmosphere of purpose and industry, even if Grim couldn't identify what, exactly, their work involved.

Most of those in the room were humans of a certain age, dressed in the simple robes of priests. That only served to make Mistress Lilith, for Grim was certain it must be her, stand out all the more. She wore a blood red dress that exposed her flesh in all the right places, while her lustrous black hair was allowed to fall to her bare shoulders. She paced slowly about the office, a presence that perhaps explained the diligent attitude of her staff. When she noticed the arrival of the elf and the ogre, her dark eyes flicked up and gazed at them. It was a gaze that spoke of power and the ability to see more than mere mortals. For while Lilith presented as a human, Grim was sure that she was, in fact, something else entirely.

'You're back,' she said to the dark elf, understandably choosing not to use his name. 'And you've brought someone—is that the right word? —else.'

'Aye. Found them on the road to Fell Towers, all ready to meet the Dark Lord and sign up as a henchman.'

'A henchman?' Lilith repeated, turning her attention to Og-Grim-Dog. 'Well, you look the part, that's for sure.' She shifted her gaze back to Simba. 'Let me hear your report first, and then I will talk to your new friend.'

Lilith led Simba to a private room in the office, leaving Og-Grim-Dog to wait amongst the priests. Grim detected a slight change to the atmosphere in the room, a barely perceptible relaxing of tension now that their mistress was no longer hovering over them—though they still appeared to be working hard at whatever it was they were doing. Og peered surreptitiously over the shoulder of one of the priests, eyeing the scrawling lines of text on the page.

Dog clutched at his belly. 'I hope they're going to feed us, whatever else they decide,' he whispered loudly.

It wasn't such a long wait before Simba exited Lilith's room and told Og-Grim-Dog it was their turn.

'It's like being back at school,' said Og, a nostalgic tone to his voice.

'You went to school?' asked the dark elf, a surprised look on his face.

'Of course,' said Og with a frown, before Grim entered Lilith's room.

'Shut the door,' she instructed from behind her desk. 'Take a seat,' she added, gesturing to a leather chair large enough to take the ogre's weight.

Grim manoeuvred himself into the chair, although Lilith remained standing on the other side of the desk.

She eyed the ogre for a while. 'So, you've come to serve the Dark Lord?'

'Yes. As a henchman,' Dog specified.

'Your name?'

'Og-Grim-Dog. A name for each of our heads, if you get my meaning.'

Lilith gave a barely perceptible nod. 'Why do you want to serve him? And how did you hear of our work here?'

'Well,' said Grim, 'in truth, the idea was suggested to us, by one of the Dark Lord's servants. Brother Kane, of Mer Khazer.'

'Brother Kane?' Lilith repeated, sounding intrigued. 'What, he found you in a dungeon?'

'We went dungeoneering with him,' Grim answered.

'You went dungeoneering with him?' She seemed fond of repeating what someone else had just said. 'I didn't know ogres were allowed to go dungeoneering.'

'We're not, anymore.'

'I see. Did you mention Brother Kane's name to the dark elf?'

'No,' said Grim. 'He said he was under cover, so we thought it best not to mention it to Simba.'

'Simba?'

'That's what I decided to call the dark elf,' Dog explained.

Lilith gave Dog a smile. 'Well, aren't you the clever one?'

'Yes,' he agreed, going a little red.

'The fact that you didn't reveal Kane's name to…Simba, is a good sign. I asked the dark elf to wait for us. He'll take you downstairs to get dinner. When the Dark Lord is ready, he will ask to speak to you. Of course, he has the final say on recruitment.'

Grim got to his feet.

'Thank you,' Dog gushed. Grim wasn't sure if it was simply down to the offer of food, or whether his brother had taken a bit of a shine to the Dark Lord's adviser.

Lilith held out a hand and awkwardly, since it required the co-operation of his brothers, Dog bent over, took her hand in his, and gave it a kiss. They left the room. Sure enough, Simba was leaning against a wall, waiting for them. The dark elf pushed himself upright and led them off, back down the curving stairs of the keep to the lower level, and then through to the refectory.

It was a large and busy place. Rows of tables and benches filled the centre of the room, while around the sides were serving counters. It was full of menials. Menials sat and ate; menials queued, waiting to be served; menials dished out the food. Grim began to get a sense of just how many servants lived and worked here.

Simba led them to the queue, from where he grabbed a tray for himself and one for Og-Grim-Dog, which Dog quickly grabbed.

Og beckoned with a finger. Understanding, Simba passed him a second tray.

'Come on,' said the dark elf. 'We have pushing in rights.'

It is not really exaggerating to describe the refectory of Fell Towers as heaven for Og-Grim-Dog. At every service counter, they were allowed to ask for whatever, and as much, as they liked. They piled their trays with cuisine from every part of Gal'azu and beyond: roast dinners from the Free Cities; dwarven cold cuts; spiced curries from the Barbarian east; halfling one-pots; pastas and breads from the Kuthenian Empire; seafood from the Pirate Isles. Og even considered trying elven salad.

When their trays were so precariously balanced that they feared dropping what they had gathered, they joined Simba at one of the tables. His eyes bulged somewhat at the sight of their dinner.

'So, tell us about your recent mission,' Grim prompted the dark elf. That way, Simba could do all the talking and they could concentrate on the eating. That would mean better odds of his brothers shovelling some of the food his way.

'I was sent to make contact with the Barbarian Resistance. I managed to establish a relationship with a cell in the town of Mer Khazer.'

Grim, Og and Dog looked at one another. Their friend Assata was a member of that cell. If their mouths hadn't been so full, one of them might have said something they perhaps shouldn't.

Grim swallowed his mouthful of shrimp, roast beef, curried lamb, tuna pasta, cold chicken and pork casserole. 'Why does the Dark Lord wish to help the Resistance?' he asked carefully.

Simba shrugged. 'They could help to destabilise the Kuthenian Empire.' He looked at three uncomprehending ogre faces. 'The Kuthenians have the most powerful realm in Gal'azu. If the Dark

Lord is going to take over the world, he'll need to destroy the Empire.'

Og-Grim-Dog relaxed. That made sense. They finished the rest of their dinner in peace. They had just begun to discuss seconds when a menial approached their table.

'Yes?' Simba asked the helmeted figure.

'A message from the Dark Lord for Og-Grim-Dog. He is ready to see you.'

A JOB INTERVIEW WITH THE DARK LORD

Og-Grim-Dog followed the menial out of the refectory. Instead of heading to the main gates of the stronghold, the menial led them to an alternative exit to the fortress. A postern gate at the rear of Fell Towers opened onto sheer cliffs, from where Grim could see and smell the ocean, and hear the waves crashing down below. He found it surprising that the Dark Lord allowed them to see this secret entrance into his stronghold. Perhaps it signified that he trusted them. Or perhaps, the Dark Lord was extremely cavalier about his security.

Grim followed the menial along the edge of the cliff. Not far ahead, he saw a figure that must be the Dark Lord. He was tall, for a human, enclosed in a heavy black cloak. He turned towards them. A horned helmet completely hid his facial features.

'The ogre, Og-Grim-Dog,' said the menial.

'Good,' said the Dark Lord, his voice rich and deep. 'Return to your duties.'

The menial left them alone with the Dark Lord. There was no doubt that he was an imposing figure, with a certain aura about him. The helmeted figure kept his face turned to them for a while, as if he was studying them, though all Grim could see behind the helmet was shadow. Eventually, the Dark Lord looked out to sea.

'I like to come out here alone,' he said at last. 'It helps me to collect my thoughts.'

Grim could think of nothing to say.

'You must need some thinking time,' said Dog. 'To plan all your evil deeds.'

Grim was pretty sure he would have come up with something better than that.

'Lilith tells me Brother Kane sent you here. You want to become one of my henchmen?'

'That's correct,' said Dog. 'I think we'd be very good at it.'

'Hmm,' said the Dark Lord as he turned to face them again, a noise that could have meant any number of things, or nothing. 'I tell you what. I will give you a test to complete before I accept you into my inner circle. It's simple enough. Perform one evil deed. Tell me about it, provide some proof or whatever, and you are in. You will likely find me here. If you can't find me, go through Lilith. Is that acceptable?'

'Of course,' Dog agreed. 'No problem. Well...we'll see you soon.'

'Very well,' said the Dark Lord. He waved a hand to dismiss them and returned his gaze to the sea.

Grim retraced their path along the cliff to the postern gate in the wall of the stronghold. He gave it a push and it swung open. 'Not even locked,' he muttered.

'Well,' said Og, an odd tone to his voice as they re-entered Fell Towers. 'Perform an evil deed, he says.'

'Shouldn't be a problem,' Dog said. 'Oi, you,' he called out to a menial walking past. 'Come over here.'

The menial dutifully changed direction and approached them.

Before Grim realised what was happening, Dog was clattering the menial over the head with his mace. As it lay sprawled out on the floor, Dog hit it one last time to make sure it was dead.

'Here we go,' he said cheerfully, returning his weapon to his belt. 'Let's take this to the Dark Lord.'

Dog picked up the corpse of the menial, and Grim dutifully turned around and returned to the postern gate, exited the stronghold and made his way back along the cliff path.

'I didn't expect you back so soon,' said the Dark Lord at their approach. His helmeted visage turned to look at the body of his dead menial, which Dog unceremoniously dumped on the ground in front of him. 'What is this?' he asked.

'An evil deed,' said Dog proudly, gesturing at the misshapen helmet of his victim, crushed inwards where his mace had struck it.

'You've killed one of my menials?' said the Dark Lord angrily. 'How is that supposed to help me?'

'You *did* ask for an evil deed,' Grim reminded him.

'Yes. Evil. Randomly killing someone isn't evil. It's psychopathic.'

'Oh,' said Dog, sounding disappointed.

'Well,' said Og, 'maybe you need to define evil a bit more clearly. Some would say it's an artificial construct anyway.'

'What nonsense,' said the Dark Lord. 'Everyone knows what evil means. The opposite of good. As the Dark Lord, it's my job to spread evil across Gal'azu.'

'So what you actually meant,' said Og, an edge to his voice, 'was to perform a deed that helps you with your goal to take over the world.'

'Yes. After all, the menials work for me—increase my power. I'm really surprised that you interpreted what I said in this way,' he said, gesturing at the dead body on the ground.

'So you're a megalomaniac?' Og asked.

Everyone looked at Og blankly.

'You're interested in power, conquering Gal'azu. That kind of thing.'

24

'Exactly,' said the Dark Lord. 'I am pleased that we understand each other now.'

'Right,' said Og, gesturing at the dead menial with a sigh. 'You know, if you keep using the word evil, this kind of thing is going to happen.'

'I suppose so,' said the Dark Lord reluctantly. 'Evil is more of a style thing, maybe. You know, I want to conquer the world in an evil fashion.'

'Whatever,' Og grumbled under his breath.

'Now he's dead,' said Dog, gesturing at the menial, 'and I'm sorry and all that, are you alright with me just chucking him in the sea?'

'I'd rather you didn't. I think he deserves a funeral of some kind. And I'm sure we can recycle his clothes. Not sure about the helmet, that's pretty banged up.'

'Well,' said Grim, 'we'll mention it needs doing to a menial. Meanwhile, we'd better get off and do our deed properly.'

'Look,' said the Dark Lord. 'Don't worry about it. It was partly my fault for not being clear. And even if you didn't do what I wanted—not remotely what I wanted—at all—it did demonstrate a certain level of commitment. Not to mention, you look really fucking evil. You're hired.'

'Really?' asked Dog enthusiastically.

'Really. Come, let me give you a little tour of Fell Towers. Then we can talk business.'

Grim followed the Dark Lord back along the cliff. Once more, they passed through the postern gate. The Dark Lord paused at the ground floor of his stronghold and Og-Grim-Dog, his new henchman, waited politely at his side. The Dark Lord ordered a group of menials to deal with their dead colleague and then turned to the ogre.

'You've been to the refectory?'

'Yes,' said Dog. 'Really good.'

'Lesson one: I like to look after my staff. The healthier and happier they are, the harder they work to achieve my goals. Free food. Free healthcare. I even pay into a pension for them. It means I have the most loyal and dedicated followers in all of Gal'azu. We win as a team, you understand?'

'Win as a team,' Dog repeated. 'I like it.'

'Well, let's head down to the basement, then. It's the most exciting part of the stronghold.'

The Dark Lord took them to a trapdoor in the floor. Two menials were on hand to lift it up for them. One of them hurried ahead down the stone steps and began to light the wall lanterns. Flickering shadows appeared as they began to descend into the murky bowels of Fell Towers. Their footsteps echoed around the basement—it was draughty, dank and chilly.

'Oh, it's lovely down here,' Dog enthused.

Even Og had to nod in agreement.

'Of course, ogres like it underground, don't you,' said the Dark Lord. 'Well, let's see if we can organise a little room for you down here.'

'That would be wonderful,' said Dog.

'Naturally,' began the Dark Lord, once they had descended to the rocky floor of his basement, 'I have given over much of the basement to dungeon cells.' He began to stroll along, past the iron bars of the first cell. It was large, big enough to hold twenty or more prisoners, but no-one was in there now.

Grim followed, keeping a respectable distance behind him, as all good henchmen do.

They passed a second cell, just as large and just as empty. 'Now,' said the Dark Lord, 'one of my favourite rooms.'

He stopped at a door. No simple bars here, it was a thick-looking slab of metal, with bolts pulled across it. The Dark Lord produced a set of keys and, squinting to find the correct one, unlocked the door.

'If you would do the honours?' he asked, stepping back.

Og and Dog slid aside the heavy bolts and opened the door. Grim followed the Dark Lord into the cell.

Inside was a single prisoner. He was chained by the ankles to one of the walls of his small cell. He was tall, which somehow made his gaunt appearance look even worse. He raised his head, squinting at the introduction of light into his cell.

'Is that you, Jonty?' the prisoner demanded.

The Dark Lord emitted an odd sounding giggle. 'Yes. I'm just showing you to one of my new henchmen.'

'Jonty?' Dog repeated.

'Yes. But make sure you never call me that. Refer to me as 'lord'.'

'Jonty, you sad little loser, let me out of here!' demanded the prisoner, with an exhausted kind of anger.

There was an unpleasant smell in the room. Grim felt sorry for the man. He had lank, long brown hair and a grimy looking beard. He looked to be in a bad way, with red sores on his skin, as well as his generally emaciated condition. But his pale blue eyes fixed on the Dark Lord with an intensity that contrasted with his physical condition.

'You're the one chained up in my cell, Fraser, so that makes you the loser,' retorted the Dark Lord with a giggle. 'Come on,' he said to Og-Grim-Dog. 'Let's get out of here.'

They left the cell, the Dark Lord locking the door and Og and Dog sliding back the bolts.

'My stupid older brother,' said the Dark Lord by way of explanation. 'Always such a precious goody-goody. Well, look at him now.'

'How long has he been in there?' Grim asked.

'A few years. At first, I thought I might have him killed, but actually it's much more fun just keeping him alive. Come on, there's something else down here I need to show you.'

Grim followed on. Dog didn't seem the least bit bothered by the Dark Lord's revelation, but he could tell that Og hadn't liked it one bit. A dark frown was fixed on his brother's face.

'I designed the pit myself,' said the Dark Lord, as they approached a wooden barrier that stopped as high as Grim's thighs. The barrier continued round in a roughly circular shape, surrounding the Dark Lord's pit. Peering over it, Og-Grim-Dog could tell that it was deep, but it was too dark to see the bottom.

The menial who had walked on ahead was busy lighting torches that were attached to the barrier.

'By the twenty-three circles of fiery Gehenna,' let out Dog. 'There's something down there. Something very large.'

Grim took a look. The torches did enough to illuminate a huge creature, wrapped about itself at the bottom of the pit.

'It's a Giant Worm from the Deserts of Karak-Tar,' said Og. 'How did you get it here?'

'Watch this!' said the Dark Lord. He grabbed a roughly forged length of metal, too crude to be called a sword, even by an ogre. He banged it against the barrier, the sound echoing around the basement. 'Come on Evie!' he called.

The worm began to move, uncoiling itself at the bottom of the pit and rising up towards the sound. It was fat as well as long—it looked far better fed than the Dark Lord's brother. Its head came into view, a giant maw of sharp teeth. As it reached them, Grim heard a strange, whistling noise coming from its mouth.

'Evie!' encouraged the Dark Lord. His pet came towards him. He then let loose with his length of metal, smashing it into the worm, once then twice, laughing as he did so. The worm's whistling became more high-pitched, before it changed course, returning to the bottom of its pit.

The Dark Lord dropped his tool to the floor as his laughter echoed around the basement—he doubled over as he tried to suck in air amid his hysterics. 'She always falls for that one,' he said, as if it was the funniest thing in the world. Tears streamed down his face. 'I told you it was exciting down here. Come on, we'll finish off the tour on the top floor.'

The Dark Lord strode off and Grim followed behind.

'This guy is a real jerk,' Og whispered into Grim's ear.

'I know,' Grim agreed. 'But Dog really likes it here.'

*

Og-Grim-Dog followed the Dark Lord to the top floor of his keep; the place that Simba the dark elf had described as the nexus of his empire.

'We'll end our tour with Lilith,' the Dark Lord said. 'But first, I have one final room to show you.'

They took one of the exits from the landing. Grim found himself walking down a richly decorated corridor: tapestries, paintings, silver candelabra, porcelain from the Kuthenian Empire. They passed doors on either side of the corridor, but the Dark Lord was heading for the room at the end, guarded by two of his menials. They saluted at his approach, and then stepped aside. Once again, the Dark Lord produced his set of keys, selecting the correct one for this door. Unlocking it, he strode in, Grim following behind.

This was a strange room. It was completely empty, save for a stand in the centre, made from figured maple wood. Grim walked over to take a look. On the stand rested a sword. Not very large, certainly by ogre standards. What made it distinctive was the material it was made from.

'Glass?' asked Dog.

'Not quite,' said the Dark Lord. 'It is made from crystal. The Sword of Samir Durg. My bane.'

'What do you mean?' Grim asked.

'The Oracle of Britrona has foretold that I cannot be killed—save by this weapon. My first instinct, once I had it in my possession, was to destroy it; bury it; send it far away. But far safer to have it here, in my possession. Under my control.'

'Is it wise to tell people about it?'

'You are my henchman now. You have my full trust. And, oughtn't you to know about the one thing that can kill me, so as to prevent my death?'

'I suppose so. You are the only one with a key to this room?'

'Indeed. Now you know the secrets of Fell Towers, it is time to put you to good use. Let us speak with Lilith. She tends to know best about which jobs best suit which individual. It liberates me—allows me to formulate my plans and ideas, without worrying about the details.'

The Dark Lord made sure that he locked the room behind them, before heading to the open plan office, where Lilith ruled over the administrators of his evil empire. Wordlessly, she led them into her private office.

'I agree with your assessment,' the Dark Lord told her. 'I have taken our newest recruit on a tour of Fell Towers.'

Lilith made a face, as if she would rather he hadn't. But she said nothing.

'Perhaps you would be able to set them up with some work? Oh, and I did offer them a room in the basement, if you can find a space?'

'Of course,' said Lilith.

'Wonderful. Well, I must be getting on.'

Lilith and Og-Grim-Dog said their farewells as the Dark Lord exited the office. The woman then stared at Og-Grim-Dog, for a long time. Grim got the impression that it was Lilith who really directed the henchmen. He wasn't sure that the Dark Lord had learned their name, or that he would remember them a couple of hours from now.

'I think it may suit you best,' she said at last, 'to spend a few days here at Fell Towers. The menials could certainly benefit from some training. That's an understatement, to be honest. When you've settled in, I will give you a proper assignment out in Gal'azu. What do you think of that?'

It sounded fine to Grim. It clearly sounded more than fine to Dog, who had the widest smile on his face that Grim had ever seen him with.

'How often are we allowed to visit the refectory?' his brother asked.

Lilith shrugged. 'As often as you like.'

An audible crack emanated from Dog's face. Grim looked at his brother. His smile had now got so wide that his jaw had locked in place. It had quickly gone from a pleasant enough sight to a rather disturbing one. Saliva began to dribble from his mouth.

'Well, thank you,' Grim said to Lilith quickly. 'I think we had better be on our way.'

She nodded absently, unable to take her eyes away from Dog's manic looking smile.

TRAINING PRECIS

'N ow then,' said the Landlord's third head, 'we were thinking you might want to try something different here.'

The Recorder paused the scratching of his quill on parchment and raised a suspicious eyebrow. 'Like what?'

'A montage,' replied the third head enthusiastically.

'What's a montage?'

'Remember, he won't have seen any movies,' the first head hissed.

The customers of The Flayed Testicles muttered uneasily to one another. If there was one thing the good people of Magidu didn't like, it was folks using words they had never heard of.

'The thing is,' began the Landlord's middle head, trying to rescue the situation, 'for the next week or so, we stayed at Fell Towers, training the Dark Lord's menials. We were hoping you would be able to write a brief account of that time, without spending too long on it.'

'Ah,' said the Recorder. 'You mean a precis.'

The ogre's three heads looked at the Recorder for a while, their expressions all furrowed brows and pursed lips. Finally, the third head responded with a sage nod.

'Yes. A pray see.'

'I agree. That should mean we can get on with it.'

The third head narrowed his eyes. 'What do you mean, 'get on with it'?'

'Well, it's just that you *did* introduce this as a dark tale.'

'And?'

'And so far, all you've really told us about is the buffet at the refectory.'

The third head spluttered indignantly. 'Oh, it gets dark, don't worry about that.'

'Fine. Then please proceed.'

'Simba soon left on some unnamed errand for the Dark Lord, and we were the only henchman at Fell Towers during that time,' began the middle head. 'There were thousands of menials living in the barracks. They manned the keep and the walls of the stronghold. They brought in food, water, timber and other supplies. At any one time, hundreds were assigned to the Dark Lord's building projects. But even though they were kept busy, the Dark Lord ensured that they also had free time reserved for them. It was in these blocks of free time that we held our training sessions. First, there was archery training.' The middle head sighed. 'We couldn't get those menials to shoot straight for love or money.'

The Recorder was bent over his parchment, busy writing his precis.

'And you have to mention guard duty,' the first head took up. 'We ran daily tests, where we would approach the gates and demand entry under a variety of pretences. One day we claimed to be a repairman; another time we said we were the milkman.'

'One day we claimed to be the Dark Lord's grandmother,' recalled the third head.

Head one nodded. 'Whatever we said, no matter how many times we told them not to, they would just open the gates and let us in.'

'Then there was what I called "pebble training",' said the third head. 'We would drop a coin or small stone or some such, a few

33

feet away from a menial. They would instantly follow the noise around a corner, or down a dark stairwell, where we could neutralise them. We tried getting them to go in pairs, or to shout a warning to their colleagues. But nothing seemed to work.'

The Recorder finished his scratching. 'So, did any of your training with the menials actually make a difference?'

'Let's just say,' said the middle head, 'that when we were called into Lilith's office, we were only too ready to be given our new assignment.'

AN OGRE IN VARENA

This is a common task given to henchmen,' Lilith explained, 'and relatively simple. Seek and destroy. Find any threats to the Dark Lord and kill them. Any children with a prophecy attached to them must be removed. Be suspicious of all orphans. Anyone with a royal heritage, bastards included. No, especially bastards. Our motto is 'if in doubt, wipe them out'. Do you understand?'

Og-Grim-Dog nodded. She had left them in little doubt.

'I'm giving you the north-western region of Gal'azu: Varena. Our influence is already strong there. No great kingdoms to interfere with your work. Sparsely populated: most settlements are isolated. In other words, this should be a success. Your assignment is finished when you have eliminated all threats. When that is done, report back here.'

*

Og-Grim-Dog was back in The Great Outside. They missed their little room in the basement of the keep at Fell Towers. Most of all, they missed the refectory. But they had been given a mission, and they were determined to fulfil it.

In his wisdom, the Dark Lord had built a road leading from Fell Towers to the region of Varena. It meant that even though the terrain about them was hard, dry and desolate, Grim was able to make good progress to the west. They made their camp by the road, feeling perfectly safe. The only people likely to be using the road as well as the ogre were the other henchmen of the Dark Lord. Grim had no real idea how many henchmen there were altogether. Neither the Dark Lord nor Lilith were willing to reveal the identities of their followers, and so the only ones he knew about were Brother Kane and Simba. Even so, he had the impression that there were not very many.

The Dark Lord's road suddenly ended, in the middle of nowhere.

'Rather odd,' said Grim.

'Maybe they ran out of materials?' Dog suggested.

'Maybe the Dark Lord is a bit clueless,' said Og. 'Who builds a road to nowhere?'

'Shut up, Og,' said Dog angrily. 'How many roads have you built?'

'None.'

'Exactly.'

'From now on,' said Grim, 'I think you two had better put your sacks on.'

Without the road, Grim found the going much slower. Streams heading north to the sea had to be traversed, and Varena was a land of hills, valleys and woods.

They were making for the Temple of Britrona. It was something of a spiritual centre for the people of Varena, since it was the home of the Oracle. Varenians of all backgrounds would visit the Temple at least once in their lifetime, with questions about their health, wealth, loved ones, or a myriad of other topics. Even simply to witness the Oracle at work. As they neared their destination, they found tracks leading to the Temple, and then the tracks became a road. It was well maintained, with other travellers making use of it, coming back and forth in equal numbers.

No doubt their precaution of wearing sacks helped them to walk through Varena without drawing too much unwanted attention. But Grim also got the impression that in the tough, rugged landscape of this region, few folks were actively looking for trouble. Beyond some stares and comments, he found that other travellers were happy to mind their own business.

It took them six days to reach the Temple of Britrona. Of course, a town had built up around the temple precincts. But it was not so big as Grim had imagined. There was little in this remote spot to provide people with a living, save for those businesses that served the visitors to the Temple. Even here, the Temple attracted a steady stream of travellers rather than huge numbers all at once. So only three inns were needed to lodge most of the visitors to the town. All the other stores you might expect to find in a moderately sized town were there, including an industrial workshop that housed the craftsmen who worked with metal, wood and leather.

But the town was only of passing interest to Og-Grim-Dog. For they were headed straight for the Temple.

*

It felt strange, to Grim, to be looking out from the Temple at the people of Varena gathered below. He felt like he should be with them: an outsider—an onlooker to the goings on at the temple. Yet here he was.

A crowd of visitors stood ready to hear the Oracle's pronouncement, townsfolk and visitors alike, all mixing together into one crowd beneath the balcony on which she stood. The Oracle's public statements came at irregular intervals, so that when she was ready to speak, everyone stopped what they were doing to listen. They gazed up at her, emotion plain to see on many faces, as they took in the figure of the greatest seer in all of Gal'azu. Grim made sure that he kept to the shadows—that he and his brothers remained unseen.

The Oracle raised her hands and a silence fell over the crowd, fearful lest they missed a word of her utterance. She was framed by tall, white marble pillars. Her red hair and white chiton blew in the wind. The clothing emphasised her purity; her proximity to the divine.

'The gods have spoken to me,' she shouted, her voice passionate, ecstatic, not far removed from sounding frenzied. 'Hear their words through me. Britrona declares that a chosen one will not come among us. The gods have not selected a hero to rise up and lead us. The Dark Lord will reign forever. Resistance is futile. That is all.'

The Oracle turned away from her listeners and left the balcony, returning to the confines of the Temple. The priests closed the doors behind her. She approached Og-Grim-Dog, her face a mask of detachment, though Grim could guess at the anger and anguish lying beneath the surface.

'You did well,' said Dog, patting the handle of his giant mace, a not so subtle reminder of the threat of violence. 'Now, we want the identities of every individual who has come to you in a vision. Be careful not to miss a single one out.'

*

Og-Grim-Dog studied their first target. It looked like the hamlet had been carved out of the forest not that long ago. In the half-light of dusk, the tiny wooden homes sat in the shadows of the tall trees. Grim thought it wouldn't take much for the forest to get its revenge and reclaim the land that had been taken from it.

'Do we really need to do this?' Og asked, as they waited for the sun to fully set.

'We weren't welcome in Mer Khazer,' Dog reminded them. 'Grim wanted to leave our cavern in Darkspike Dungeon. We were lost and lonely in that swamp. So, yes. This is the price we pay for our free room and full board at Fell Towers.'

Neither Og nor Grim could argue with that.

They approached the homes under the cover of darkness. Less chance of being seen—more chance that everyone was at home.

Once the killing started, they wasted no time, moving quickly from house to house, not giving the humans a chance to gather their wits and put up a fight. It was a family they were after—one that moved from place to place in the wilds of Varena. In particular, a young boy, said to have been born with incredible magical powers. His parents had done their best to protect him, but their luck had run out this night.

Grim was an ogre. He wasn't squeamish when it came to the slaying of enemies. Nonetheless, the murder of children, even human ones, wasn't his favourite pastime, and he was glad that it was Dog who did the work that night rather than him. The mace finished them quickly enough. Og had his pike in hand, but he took no part in the killings either, insisting that his role was to defend them from any surprise attacks.

'That must be them,' Og said when Dog was done.

'Looked very much like the Oracle's description,' Grim agreed.

'Probably,' said Dog, 'but we need to make sure.'

'Come on, Dog,' Og argued. 'We're better off leaving now.'

'What if a witness to this slaughter turns against the Dark Lord?' Dog countered. 'Or spreads the word to others? No, we need to complete our task. 'If in doubt, wipe them out'. Remember?'

Dog had his way and there was little left of the homes when they were done. The forest would soon swallow the rest up; and it would be like the hamlet and the people who had lived there had never existed.

A BITE TO EAT AT THE PRESSED APPLES

After the attack on the hamlet, Og-Grim-Dog travelled south-west. They had topped up their supplies from their victims' food stores, but nonetheless, it was hard going for Grim.

Then it got worse.

It was on the third day that he smelt them.

'Trolls,' he warned his brothers.

Even Og woke up alert at that warning. His brothers sniffed the air as Grim quickened his pace.

'I reckon three of them. Probably all males,' said Dog.

'Agreed,' said Og. 'And not that far behind us. Now they have our scent, they'll not give up the hunt unless we leave their territory.'

'I'll never outrun them,' said Grim. 'And we don't know the area well enough to get to safety.'

'Then we don't have long to make a plan,' said Dog.

*

Og-Grim-Dog stood in the forest glade. It was a pretty enough spot, covered in pine needles and crunchy brown leaves. Not a bad place for them to meet their pursuers. Dog had his mace ready and Og his pike. At the very least, they would see them coming.

They came into sight at last. They were unhurried, making their way through the trees. Three young males, not the kind of group to give up the chase or turn away from a fight. Each carried the huge wooden clubs favoured by their kind. With their long, powerful arms, a single strike from such a weapon would disable their enemy.

They entered the ogre's glade and the smell of them came with them. There was little emotion on their faces—Grim saw no pleasure that their quarry had been chased down, or excitement at the prospect of a fight. The lead troll made a snarl, which at least livened up his flat, brute of a face. The other two—his brothers, most likely—spread out a little on either side of him. They knew that they had the advantage. Three clubs striking from three different angles would prove to be too much for one ogre in the end. They would have to take care that Og or Dog didn't get in an early blow; but otherwise, everything was in their favour.

Og-Grim-Dog didn't move. They didn't speak. They just waited as, slowly and deliberately, the three trolls closed in.

Then the one on the right disappeared. Its front foot had gone down on one of their traps, concealed by fallen leaves, and it was too clumsy to prevent its forward momentum from carrying it down into the pit. A bellow of pain was a welcome confirmation that it had landed on a spike or two down there.

That shifted the odds nicely. Two trolls against one ogre wasn't such an easy win. And they now had an injured third who they might want to help. The remaining two looked at Og-Grim-Dog. A tiny flash of anger crossed their faces, but their dull expressions soon returned. They knew they had lost their quarry this time. There would be others.

'So long,' Og offered them cheerily, before Grim turned away.

✲

'At last, a road of sorts,' commented Grim, as he cut onto a muddy path.

Days of walking through the wilderness had taken their toll, though mercifully they had faced no more trolls, or other enemies.

'Will it lead us to the town, do you think?' Dog asked.

'I hope so.'

'What was it called again?'

'Yeggton. A town of thieves, rogues and other criminals, by all accounts.'

'A thieves' town? Ridiculous.'

'What do you mean?'

'Well, how can you have a town of thieves? Are they all constantly stealing from one another? Where does the food come from to feed a town of thieves? If you were a farmer, would you sell your produce at a town full of thieves? Are there no shopkeepers, craftsmen and the like? It just doesn't make any sense.'

'You always have to ruin everything, don't you Dog?'

Even if Yeggton wasn't inhabited solely by thieves, The Pressed Apples was as rough a watering hole as you might find in all of Gal'azu. Mean looking men, and meaner looking women, stared at one another in between swilling down the piss-flavoured excuse of a brew, waiting for an excuse to begin larruping one another.

When Dog accidentally on purpose knocked someone's pint, it all kicked off. Soon chairs were flying across the room and drinks were smashing over heads. By that point, Og-Grim-Dog had already identified their target by his tattoos.

An ex-soldier by the name of Karlens Stone, fallen on hard times since the death of his family, he had been drowning his sorrows in his cups for the last five years. But if he ever sobered up, he was just the kind of hard-bitten hero with nothing to lose who might take on the Dark Lord.

Well, that wasn't going to happen. Amid the chaos of the bar room brawl, he suddenly found his head held in place by an ogre hand. Bleary with beer, he was unable to react before his neck was bitten open by what looked like a giant wolf. By the time his death had been noticed, the ogre who had started the fray was long gone.

*

In this manner, Og-Grim-Dog toured across Varena, locating and eliminating everyone on the list of potential threats they had extracted from the Oracle. When they were done, autumn was turning into winter, and it was a cold, hard journey back to Fell Towers. Keeping them going was the thought of a visit or two to the refectory.

At last, the thin, finger-like towers of the Dark Lord's stronghold appeared on the horizon. It was enough to give Grim a final boost of energy. As he dragged them towards the tall gates of Fell Towers, he couldn't help but notice a new building had been erected a short distance from the gates.

'Sheev's?' he asked out loud.

Sure enough, the new building had a sign out front with the same name as the eatery that Raya the elf had introduced them to in Mer Khazer.

'Smells like Sheev's,' said Dog.

Indeed, the smell of spiced meat was unmistakeably the same.

'Are we popping in for a chilli burger and fries, then?' asked Og.

44

'Humph.'

'What is it, Dog?'

'It's just that I had my heart set on the refectory in the keep.'

'Right you are, Dog,' Grim agreed. 'We can always visit Sheev's another time. I wonder what it's doing here?'

'It's obviously popular already,' Og noted.

A steady stream of menials walked back and forth between Sheev's and the open gates of Fell Towers.

Grim followed two menials who were making their way back to the stronghold. They each clutched a little wooden figurine, which presumably they had received from Sheev's.

'Who did you get?' one of them asked their companion.

'Larik the Bludgeoner.'

'Me too. Already got him. I was really hoping for Reginald Shit-Blood.'

Grim continued, completely unchallenged, through the gates and into the stronghold. It wasn't until he got to the keep that there was any kind of attempt to police who came and went. Four menials stood by the entrance. As Grim approached, Dog knocked on one of the helmets with his big knuckles.

'Let us in, menials!' he demanded.

The door was opened for them and Grim strode through.

'Food first?' Dog suggested. 'Then we can give our report.'

FOOD FOR THOUGHT

T he Dark Lord wishes to see you in the Throne Room,' the menial told them.

'D'ya think we can finish dinner first?' Dog asked.

It hadn't taken long to fill their trays up with food. The refectory was much quieter, since many menials now dined at Sheev's instead.

The menial made a dubious expression which suggested that wasn't a very good idea.

'Perhaps we'd better go straight away,' said Grim. 'We can always come back after, can't we?'

Grim got to his feet and they followed the menial out of the refectory and across to the other side of the keep.

'We've never been invited to the Throne Room before,' Og noted.

More menials guarded the door, but they opened it upon the ogre's approach. Grim kept walking. The Throne Room was long, meaning he had to walk to the far end of the room, where the Dark Lord was seated upon his throne. Lilith stood next to him, while Grim walked between two rows of menials who stood to attention along the edges of the room.

Grim stopped in front of the Dark Lord. Unsure what to do, he decided to get down on one knee.

'The Dark Lord wishes to hear your report in person, henchman,' Lilith informed them.

Between them, the three brothers recounted their exploits in Varena.

'Well done!' said the Dark Lord when they were done. 'I knew you would be a good choice. With Varena and the other regions of Gal'azu subdued, it is finally time for us to go on the offensive!'

'What will that involve?' Og dared to ask.

'Taking on our greatest enemy, of course: The Kuthenian Empire. I have developed the perfect plan.' The Dark Lord pointed at Og-Grim-Dog. 'Maybe you thought those cliff walks were a waste of time, eh? Well listen to this. We kidnap the Emperor's daughter, bring her here, and I marry her. That gives me a claim to the Jade Throne. If the Emperor tries to send an army here to take her back, we crush it. If not, he looks weak, his grip on power starts to crumble, and I assert my claim.'

Dog puffed out his cheeks. 'Well, that *does* sound very clever.'

'Are we going to be involved in this?' Og asked.

'You will be sent to the Empire to bring Princess Borte back here.'

Lilith cleared her throat. 'No offence to Og-Grim-Dog intended. But it is a dangerous assignment you have set him. Should he fail, then what?'

'I have another henchman lined up if something were to befall the ogre.'

'And should he fail as well?'

'Then I have the perfect replacement to send in his stead.'

'So, just an idea,' said Lilith. 'Why not send these henchmen together? Between them, they may have a greater chance of carrying out the plan.'

'Hmm. Interesting suggestion. She's not just a pretty face, is she?' the Dark Lord asked Og-Grim-Dog, jabbing a thumb in Lilith's direction.

By ogre standards, Lilith wasn't in the least bit attractive. But Og-Grim-Dog felt obliged to nod along enthusiastically.

'Well, that's certainly worth considering,' the Dark Lord conceded. 'Any questions, ogre?'

'I was wondering about Sheev's,' said Dog. 'Why have they moved here now?'

'Sheev's have opened a new premises here,' Lilith explained. 'They still have their old place in Mer Khazer.'

'Hmm,' said Dog, digesting that fact. 'Two Sheev's, eh? A bit like Discount Dungeon Supplies.'

'What do you know about them?' Lilith asked sharply.

'They have more than one store, too,' Dog explained. 'There's one in Mer Khazer. And we visited another in Wight's Hollow.'

'Yes, well. The reality is, we have to be prepared to work with big suppliers like these,' said Lilith.

'What about the refectory?' Dog asked, worried. 'I mean, I have nothing against Sheev's, their chilli burgers are out of this world. But the refectory is special, too.'

'I agree,' said the Dark Lord. 'The refectory gives everyone a healthy and filling square meal, for free. But it seems like the menials would rather pay to get a meal from Sheev's. I want my workers to be happy, and free to spend their wages how they like. But still—'

The Dark Lord sounded a little anguished about the situation.

Lilith sighed. 'But we also want to raise an army, don't we? If we are sending thousands of menials against the Kuthenians, we need to pull them out of other occupations. Closing the kitchens would be one way to do that.'

'No! Don't say that!' Dog cried. 'There must be another way?'

'We haven't decided anything yet,' the Dark Lord said quickly, apparently trying to assuage Dog's dismay.

Lilith looked cross. 'That will be all, Og-Grim-Dog. You did well in Varena. But let's be clear. Operational decisions are not your concern.'

Og-Grim-Dog resisted for as long as they could, but after a few days they found themselves at Sheev's.

'We'll switch back to the refectory tomorrow,' Grim assured Dog as they took their food to a booth.

He sat them down and his brothers got to work unwrapping their meal.

'What's the toy?' he asked them.

Og picked it up to show him. It was a figurine of an elven archer. Og read the lettering at the base of the figure out loud.

'Raya Sunshine.'

'Appropriate, I suppose,' Grim said, 'since she was the one who took us to Sheev's. I do miss her.'

A menial leaned over the partition separating the next booth along.

'Did I hear you say you got Raya Sunshine? Do you want to swap for Larik the Bludgeoner?'

Dog punched the menial in the head, sending him sprawling back over the partition onto his own table.

'No.'

OLD ACQUAINTANCES

The next day, Og-Grim-Dog was invited back to the Throne Room. A third figure was with The Dark Lord and Lilith. All three brothers gasped as they recognised him.

'Gurin Fuckaxe,' Dog let out.

The dwarf fixed them with a grumpy stare.

'What are you doing here?' Dog asked.

'Well, my options were somewhat limited when you had me arrested back in Mer Khazer. Remember?'

'Oh, yes. Now you mention it.'

'Anyway, I work for the Dark Lord now. I didn't know you'd be here, but I guess it figures. The Bureau of Dungeoneering has seen fit to exclude your kind as well, after all.'

'I didn't know you two had met before,' said Lilith. 'It's our policy not to reveal the identities of our henchmen. Is this going to be a problem?'

'Not for us,' said Dog.

Gurin shrugged. 'We worked well together before, for the most part. Don't see why we can't again.'

'Good,' said the Dark Lord. 'Because I've decided to entrust you both with my most important plan. Working together, you will infiltrate Pengshui, the capital of the Kuthenian Empire. There, you will abduct the Emperor's daughter, Borte, from the palace and bring her—unharmed—here.'

'I have organised for you to meet with two more of our operatives,' said Lilith, 'who will take part in the assignment with you. They will be waiting for you a week from now, at a pre-agreed location. If they don't make it there, proceed without them.'

'I suppose you're not going to tell us who in Gehenna they are?' asked Gurin.

'Correct. If they're there, you'll know them.'

'And who's in charge of this little trip?' pursued the dwarf.

Lilith shrugged. 'I'm sure you'll work that out amongst yourselves. All henchmen are of equal rank in the Dark Lord's chain of command.'

The Dark Lord nodded gravely at this. 'I cannot stress enough how important this mission is to me. Succeed, and you will be bringing the Dark Lady to Fell Towers.'

Grim stole a glance at Lilith, wondering what she made of her leader using such a title for someone else. Her dark eyes gazed back, revealing nothing.

✳

Gurin and Og-Grim-Dog left by the same road they had used when they had first arrived at Fell Towers. They were loaded up with provisions, which went some way to make up for exchanging the comfort of Fell Towers for the biting wind and driving rain of the Great Outside.

Still, there weren't many creatures abroad in Gal'azu tougher than the dwarf and the ogre, and they made stubborn progress, regardless of the weather. There was little talk. There was an awkwardness between them after the events of Mer Khazer. The fact that the wind soon stole away one's words was a fine excuse

51

not to bother speaking, and after a day's travel in such conditions, they were ready for sleep.

Several days passed like this until one evening, with a fire going in the shelter of a cave, they spoke at last.

'Raya wrote us,' said Og, warming his hand by the fire. 'Said there was another dwarf in Mer Khazer, who rescued you.'

'Aye. Maurin was in Mer Khazer, recently come back from a dungeon crawl of his own. He sprung us from Hassletoff's cell.'

'Then what?' Dog asked.

'What do you mean, then what? Then nothing.'

'Wondered how you ended up working for the Dark Lord.'

'Humph. Could ask you the same question.'

'It was made clear we weren't welcome in Mer Khazer,' said Grim. 'We went back to our dungeon for a while. But I'd been given a taste of something more after our time with the Bureau. I persuaded my brothers to leave.'

'You fancied the life of a hero, eh? How did that work out for you?' Gurin asked, not hiding the bitterness from his voice.

'We ended up in the Swamp.'

The dwarf laughed at that—a surprising sound, but a welcome one.

'And from there, to Fell Towers,' Grim added, leaving out the role of Brother Kane.

'They sent us into Varena,' said Dog, taking up the story. 'Eliminating any threats to the Dark Lord.'

Dog said it with a note of pride, but Grim didn't need to look at his other brother to know there would be shame on his face.

'Aye. Been doing similar work as you, down in the south,' said Gurin quietly. 'From heroes to villains, eh? Not a comfortable step to take.'

'Surely you had other options,' said Og. It was part statement, part question.

'Of course I did. I could have left Gal'azu. There's always work to be had in the mines of the Ferric Hills. But this old dwarf is too stuck in his ways. Too used to his independence and too fond of swinging his axe. I don't pretend there was any honour in the choice I made.'

'And what did the Dark Lord demand of you to test your loyalty?' asked Og.

'That's between me and him, don't you think?' asked Gurin. 'I don't reveal the identities of other henchmen and I don't ask them the price they paid.' The dwarf pulled his blanket about him. 'No doubt you think it strange that I stick to these rules when I've broken every other principle I ever held. But there it is.'

✻

Gurin was ever one for taking the lead, and Og-Grim-Dog was content to allow the dwarf to decide on the route. It therefore came as something of a surprise when he announced that they were closing in on the meeting point.

'Dorwich City,' he said, pointing to the outline of a large settlement that was almost obscured by the sheets of rain that continued to pelt them mercilessly.

'Hmm, that name sounds familiar,' said Dog.

'We were chased by the reeve of Dorwich City and his posse,' Grim reminded him. 'A man by the name of Deston. We fought them outside Mer Khazer.'

'I don't recall a fight outside Mer Khazer,' claimed Og.

'Well, it *happened*,' said Grim impatiently. 'Only last year.'

'There's not going to be trouble, is there?' Gurin asked. 'They tend to take law and order quite seriously in Dorwich.'

'Not sure,' Grim admitted. 'When we parted, the reeve indicated that we had an understanding. That said, he did have Og's pike at his throat at the time.'

Gurin sighed. 'That doesn't exactly fill me with confidence. But there's little point in trying to sneak around the city with a three-headed ogre in tow. We'll just have to see what kind of reception we get.'

Dorwich had substantial city walls. It told Grim two things. First, the city was able to defend itself. Second, there were things inside that were worth defending. Rising above the walls was the spire of the cathedral. No doubt some of the things worth defending were in there.

The guards at the city gates all made the same kind of face as the dwarf and the ogre joined the queue for entry into Dorwich. It was an expression that said they weren't sure what was about to happen, but they understood that the odds of it being a good thing were low.

'You might as well just wait to one side,' one of the older guards hollered at them. 'We're going to need someone with authority to have their say before we let you in.'

It was a reasonable enough request, and the two henchmen waited patiently as the human visitors to the city were waved through.

'Uh-oh,' said Grim at last. He instantly recognised the figure of Deston, the reeve of the city, who had arrived on the scene. He recognised the muscular frame, the aura of confidence that comes from other men doing exactly what you tell them to do. 'Crunch time.'

Deston spoke briefly with his guards and then approached. He smiled at them both.

'We meet again, ogre. And this time you have a dwarf for a companion. Rather unusual visitors, even for a cosmopolitan place such as this.'

'We're just passing through,' Gurin commented.

'Indeed. I have been told to expect your arrival. You are welcome in Dorwich. Though please make sure that just passing through is all you end up doing.'

'Will do,' said Grim.

Deston waved at his guards and they stood aside to let the pair through.

'You may want to visit The Cracked Nuts while you're here,' the reeve called after them. 'Down by the river.'

'The Cracked Nuts,' Gurin repeated. 'Got it.'

They made their way into Dorwich with urgency, as if they didn't trust the reeve not to change his mind. Stares met them as they walked past, but Og-Grim-Dog was used to worse than that.

'I've been told to expect your arrival, he said,' Grim muttered. 'Does that mean Deston is working for the Dark Lord, too?'

'Who knows?' said Gurin. 'It wouldn't surprise me.'

'Is anyone *not* working for the Dark Lord?' Og wondered rhetorically.

Finding the river was easy enough. It was busy, the city's position on the waterway tempting traders to come with wares from all over Gal'azu. There were docks for loading and unloading, all busy with men carrying items that had just been bought or were being delivered for sale. Elsewhere, manufactories churned out textiles and other goods in huge numbers, that could be packed onto barges and sold for profit. They walked past a branch of

Discount Dungeon Supplies, that appeared to be doing a brisk trade amongst foreigners and citizens alike.

With all this industry and so many people working in such a small space, it was no surprise that several inns were able to flourish with a riverside location. Gurin and Og-Grim-Dog marched along the riverbank until they found the one they were after.

The Cracked Nuts was quiet and nearly empty, but it looked like the kind of place that would get very busy in the evening.

They made their way to the bar, looking around for the signs of a familiar face.

'It would be a lot easier if we knew who we were looking for,' Gurin complained.

Grim noticed the man at the bar looking at them with an alarmed expression. 'We don't want no trouble here,' he said.

'It's alright,' came a voice from behind them. 'They're with me.'

Og-Grim-Dog and Gurin turned around at the same time.

Four mouths dropped open.

'Assata?'

EAST

Og-Grim-Dog had never had the luxury of three pillows before. It really was quite something, and they each agreed that they had woken more rested than they could remember.

They were travelling downriver on a barge transporting textiles. The cargo on board meant that there was a selection of comfortable items upon which they could rest their heads, and they had taken full advantage.

With them were Gurin, Assata and Simba. Assata and Simba had arrived in Dorwich City together, with instructions to wait for the dwarf and the ogre. Wasting no time, they had booked passage for the group on the barge. They had left the city the day after Og-Grim-Dog and Gurin had arrived.

It was a surprise, to Grim, to find Assata working for the Dark Lord. Much more so than Gurin. Thinking back, he remembered Simba telling them that he had made contact with the Barbarian Resistance in Mer Khazer. Maybe if he had recalled that comment, he would have been less surprised to see Assata in Simba's company.

It was a decidedly pleasant experience for Grim, watching the world go by from the comfort of the boat. No need to move his tired legs anymore; no marching through a rainstorm. When the weather was bad, they simply huddled under a bolt of cloth. When it was clear, he could gaze out at the countryside on each bank, or follow the activities of the birds and other animals who lived on the river.

Since they were heading downstream, the boatmen who manned the craft were having an easy time of things, too. The Auster was wide and strong at this point in its course, and often they had little to do themselves. When the wind blew against them severely, they would prod long poles into the riverbed and push the barge along. For the most part, the crew seemed to be seasoned travellers who had seen their share of oddities over their years of roving. Only a few continued to gawp at the three-headed ogre, and the white-haired dark elf.

Og-Grim-Dog's companions appeared to share the same sense of calm, at least on the surface. Grim couldn't say for sure what Gurin and Assata told themselves about their association with the Dark Lord. Then, there was the question of their assignment once they got to Kuthenia. Surely there couldn't be many tasks more dangerous than abducting the daughter of the most powerful ruler in all of Gal'azu. But no-one seemed anxious to discuss the task. No-one seemed particularly eager to talk at all, and Grim didn't mind that one bit.

It was therefore some days before Og-Grim-Dog found themselves alone with Assata and engaged in a proper conversation. She told them about her latest dungeon crawl, with Sandon, Raya, Brother Kane and a couple of new recruits. It sounded like little had changed at the Bureau, and that the takings from the dungeons remained meagre. Still, Grim couldn't stop a pang of envy from appearing, that his friends went on their adventure without him.

Assata then listened with a keen interest when they described Fell Towers to her. Grim told her about the oversized gates, the dark granite buildings and the thin towers rising up to the sky. He explained who the menials were and what they did. Og told her about his impressions of the Dark Lord; about his pet, Evie, and his brother, Fraser, both kept in the basement. He mentioned Lilith's role in the organisation. Finally, Dog spent a not inconsiderable time exhaustively listing all the food items available in the refectory.

'How did Simba convince you to serve the Dark Lord?' Og finally asked.

Assata looked about them for prying ears before she answered.

'Let's get one thing straight. I don't serve the Dark Lord. I'm working for the Resistance. I'm doing this for all my people still held in bondage in the Empire.'

'How will this help them?'

'If we succeed in—' she paused, looking about them again. 'If we succeed in our mission, the repercussions for the Kuthenian Empire could be severe. A war with the Dark Lord, even. At the least, the weakening of the monarchy and the ruling class. The more instability and unrest, the more chance for the Resistance to lead a rebellion. There are enough slaves in the Empire to rise up and slit the throats of their masters. We could destroy Kuthenia from within.'

Grim thought about it. *You could do the Dark Lord's work for him.*

＊

They travelled down the Auster until it swung south on its way to the coast. The bargemen would follow the river all the way to the great port of Avolo, where they could sell their cargo for an easy profit. For the Dark Lord's henchmen, however, their route lay east. To Pengshui, capital of the Empire.

A large town by the name of Linby had grown up at this point in the river. Dropped at the wharf, the three henchmen and the barbarian investigated their options for heading east. Their two concerns were transporting someone of Og-Grim-Dog's size, and drawing as little attention to themselves as possible. Money was not an issue, since the Dark Lord had provided them with ample expenses to get his assignment done.

In the end, all of them agreed that their best option was to buy a cart pulled by horses. Assata and Gurin went off to select the best one: she to check on the health of the animals, while Gurin was keen to haggle over the price. That left Og-Grim-Dog and Simba to tour the stalls, restocking their provisions. Because of its location, Linby had an enticing mix of cuisine from west, east and south, and Og-Grim-Dog were in their element. The smell of spiced meat led them to a side street, where they discovered another branch of Sheev's.

'Seem to be spreading everywhere, don't they?' Og noted.

'No surprise, I suppose,' said Grim. 'What's not to like?'

Dog slavered in agreement, but Og had his thinking face on.

'Should we buy some for our journey?' asked Simba.

'Does a bugbear shit in the woods?' asked Dog.

When they were done and had located the others, the dwarf and barbarian had already made their choice, parted with their money and were ready to go. Gurin declared himself to be the least conspicuous of the group and argued that he should take the reins. Since this meant they got to sit in relative comfort inside the coach, no-one else was minded to quarrel with him.

A decent looking road led out of Linby and with little trouble they found themselves heading east.

*

The decent looking road didn't last for very long. Despite the fact that this was a key route between the west and east of Gal'azu, it passed through a land claimed by many, but in practice, ruled by none. The absence of a ruler or body politic of any kind meant there was no-one to maintain the road. Combined with the fact that they were travelling in winter, the road soon deteriorated into a churned, muddy mess.

It was Og-Grim-Dog who suffered the most from the poor state of the highway. First, every time the wheels of the cart got stuck, the ogre had to get out and push it free. Second, it was decided that one of the reasons the cart kept getting stuck was because they were in it. The solution, of course, was for the ogre to get out and walk.

Grim, therefore, would watch the cart trundle off into the distance, while he had to walk through the mud and puddles. Occasionally, he would catch back up with it—Og and Dog would free it from the mire once more—then they'd watch it disappear into the distance again.

This was the way in which the group approached the border of the Kuthenian Empire. As they drew closer and closer, so they began to discuss what their strategy should be once they passed into enemy territory.

'If barbarians are slaves in the Empire,' Gurin mused as he prodded at the night fire they sat about with a stick, 'we could pretend to be slavers, or some such, bringing Assata for sale.'

'Ha!' Simba enthused. 'We could march straight to the capital!'

'So, we're slavers,' said Og, examining the idea, 'who have come all the way to Kuthenia, with only one slave.'

'Maybe she escaped, and we're bounty hunters,' said the dwarf, amending his plan. He looked around at his campmates. No-one except the dark elf looked impressed. 'Alright, I'm just thinking out loud here, no need to look like I just broke wind at your mother's funeral.'

'The truth is,' said Assata, 'that the four of us are simply too conspicuous to go wandering about freely in the Kuthenian Empire. The culture there is a lot more closed than you are used to in the west: there simply aren't that many foreigners. The only way we are going to get anywhere is to make contact with the Resistance. We have associates all over the country, and most slaves are sympathetic to our cause. We must rely on them to get us to Pengshui.'

'Excellent!' declared Simba, equally as sold on the idea as he had been on Gurin's. 'And once we get to the capital, the palace slaves could lead us straight to the princess!'

'So we just approach the first slave we come across?' Gurin asked doubtfully.

'Nearly. *I* approach them.'

'And what if they give us up to their masters? You may find that your Resistance isn't as universally loved as you like to think.'

'I'm aware that there are risks. But we don't have a better plan.'

True enough, thought Grim.

In a lawless land where no-one rules, the scourge of bandits is as inevitable as flies on freshly laid shit.

More surprising, was that a gang of them chose to rob this particular group. Perhaps, as they approached in the darkness, surrounding the small camp, and outnumbering their victims twenty to four, they believed the odds were firmly in their favour.

As it was, the dark elf had heard their approach well in advance. Og-Grim-Dog's night vision wasn't quite in the same league as Simba and Gurin's, but like his two friends they had an advantage over humans. They waited, Gurin and Simba under the cart, Og-

Grim-Dog behind a pile of rocks. Assata sat by the fire, next to three bedrolls, giving the impression that a single enemy was on watch.

When the first scream reached him, Grim knew his friends had left their hiding spot and it was time for him to do the same. Figures loomed in the gloom, some tip-toeing forwards, others rooted to the spot at the sound of a dark elf shouting an incomprehensible, yet sinister, challenge into the night. There was something about the dark elf's native language that made Grim's hackles rise, and when it was accompanied by the agonised screams of his victims, he didn't blame those bandits who hesitated one bit.

Og's pike was perfect for an encounter such as this. By the time the bandits saw three ogre faces emerge from the dark, eighteen feet of wood and steel was already on its way. While Og was reluctant to carry out the Dark Lord's dirty work, he didn't object to purging men such as this, and a handful fell to his polearm in short order.

The bandits broke when they realised how badly their plan had gone awry. Og-Grim-Dog let them go—unlike the dark elf, who followed them into the night, calling to them in the godforsaken language of his people.

INFILTRATION OF THE EMPIRE PRECIS

The Landlord paused his storytelling, and his three heads looked at one another. A particularly observant customer may have noticed these looks and concluded that all three heads looked a little unsure of themselves.

The Recorder ceased his scratching and looked up. 'What? Another 'montage'?'

The third head frowned at him. 'It's just that it's hard to tell the story of the next few weeks.'

'How so?'

'We entered the Empire,' the middle head explained, 'and Assata made contact with the Resistance, just as she had wanted. They were all slaves, working in the fields or houses of their Kuthenian masters. They took us in, gave us shelter, shared their food with us. Then they would take us to the next farm, or the next village, and pass us on to another group of slaves. That was how we were able to travel across Kuthenia, unseen by the authorities.'

'I see. But why is it hard to tell that story?'

'Well,' began the first head, 'we only ever saw the inside of barns. Assata did all the talking. During the day, we slept. We moved at night, in the dark. We had no idea where we were going—totally reliant on our guides, who knew the land we passed through. They arranged to make the swap at some location—a mound, or a copse of trees—and then we would be taken straight to the next hideout. Days and then weeks went by, and we barely saw a thing or spoke a word to anyone.'

'Alright then,' said the Recorder. 'Another precis. When did this routine end?'

'It wasn't until we got to the capital. Pengshui.'

'I see,' said the Recorder. He absently stroked the feathered end of his quill on the parchment, while drumming the fingers of his other hand onto the desk.

Three pairs of ogre eyes looked at this display for a while, until they could hold their tongues no longer.

'Come on, out with it,' said the Landlord's first head. 'I can tell something's up.'

'Well—yes. Something's been bothering me. It's the matter of the Dark Lord's test of loyalty, for his new henchmen. Rumours abound of the crimes he demanded of fresh recruits, to prove their commitment to his cause. You told us that Gurin the dwarf would not speak of the price he paid. And yet, when it came to your turn, the Dark Lord apparently let you off.'

The Landlord's third head frowned at the man. '*Let us off?* That's not what we said at all. We killed a menial for him. I hope you're not forgetting things.'

Now it was the Recorder's turn to look offended. 'I do not *forget things*.' He scanned his piece of parchment. 'These are the words you gave to the Dark Lord—and I quote. "Don't worry about it. It was partly my fault for not being clear." Now that sounds very much like it was letting you off. And, in all honesty, it doesn't sound very much like the Dark Lord to me.'

'What are you getting at?' demanded the middle head angrily. 'Are you insinuating that we are lying?'

The Recorder sighed. 'I'm just checking that the story I have is correct. You will recall that I pledged to sift the facts from the fabrications. I don't fully understand why the Dark Lord would spare you from a monstrous deed, and you alone.'

'But you see,' said the middle head calmly, 'we are telling you *our* story. The motives of the other actors cannot always be known with certainty by us. If you are asking me to speculate why the Dark Lord didn't require a monstrous deed of us, it was perhaps because he already knew us to be a monster. Does one ask a dwarf whether they can wield an axe, or a recorder whether they can write?'

The Recorder held up his hands. 'Very well. It is as you say. The motives of the Dark Lord may never be known for sure. No offence intended. Please, continue.'

PENGSHUI

Og-Grim-Dog, his friends and a few members of the Resistance, stood in the half-light of dawn.

The mighty walls of Pengshui loomed before them. They looked impregnable. But looks, it turned out, could be deceiving.

'We have a way in,' Assata declared.

'How?' asked Grim.

Assata nodded to the man next to her. Referred to as Little El, he was a local leader in the Resistance. He was short and muscular, with swirling, ink black symbols on his meaty forearms.

He gestured ahead, to an inconspicuous looking group of farm buildings. 'There's a tunnel that goes under the walls.'

Gurin looked suspicious. 'Built by who, and why?'

'It's used to smuggle goods into the city,' said Little El.

'Controlled by a bunch of criminals, then.'

'It ain't a crime to deny taxes to this vicious, murderous regime,' Little El retorted.

The other members of the Resistance reacted as well, staring at the dwarf with animosity. Assata looked worried.

We could do without a fight right now, Grim said to himself.

Gurin shrugged. 'Assume I don't care about your politics. Is it safe?'

Little El studied Gurin for a while, saying nothing, before he relented.

'The Resistance helped build it. We get to use it. We can get you in and back out via the tunnel with no questions asked.'

'Alright. Let's do it then.'

'We're getting you in,' Little El added. 'But don't expect us to help with the rest of it. That's your job.'

'Don't worry about that,' Simba spoke up. 'We can handle the extraction.'

Little El looked at the dark elf, then at Gurin and Og-Grim-Dog. He nodded. 'Very well. We need to get you in now, before the city fully wakes.'

If the tunnel was a little cramped for a human, it was barely navigable for an ogre. It wasn't that Og-Grim-Dog had a fear of enclosed spaces. It was simply that their physical dimensions didn't match up to the size of the shaft they had to squeeze through. Arms, legs and back got scraped as they crawled and slithered their way along. Grim lost count of the number of times he had to tell Dog to keep his voice down, as his brother voiced his discomfort and frustration with shouts and protracted swearing. But in the end, somehow, they found themselves clambering out into a brick-walled and earthen-floored storeroom. Wooden barrels were stacked at one end, most likely rolled through the tunnel to avoid the imperial tariffs.

Grim leaned against a wall, pulling in lungfuls of air as sweat trickled down his body.

'It's best if you stay in here today,' Little El advised them. 'When the sun goes down, we can take you out and show you the palace.'

None of them considered arguing. It had been another long night of travelling, and the tunnel had just about finished them off. They needed sleep—needed their wits about them, if they were going to infiltrate the imperial palace and get out alive.

✻

Og-Grim-Dog awoke to the smell of food. The Resistance had provided dinner: mountains of rice, with fish and meat and vegetables stirred in.

'Don't eat too much,' Assata warned them as they began to tuck in. 'We need you alert, not half asleep from a full stomach.'

Dog barked with laughter at what he assumed was a joke.

Fed and rested, Grim felt much better about the task waiting for them tonight. It had taken them months to get to this point, and soon it would be all over, one way or another. He could feel the adrenaline building, the grip of anticipation in his gut. But Little El told them they had to wait a while longer.

'The day is waning,' he told them. 'But I'll not risk moving you 'til it's full dark.'

They waited. There was not much to discuss or plan until they saw the palace for themselves. They checked their weapons one last time. Assata had her sword, and Gurin his axe. Simba had two swords, that both ended in a wicked looking curve. Og had his pike and Dog his mace. Grim, of course, had no weapons, since he had no hands. Strange. He'd had his whole life to get used to it. But even now, watching the others sharpening their blades with a whetstone, he still wished that he was doing the same.

At last, it was time to move out. Little El was their only guide.

'We want to keep our numbers down,' he explained, as they exited the brick building onto a large yard that held a number of similar units. 'We're conspicuous enough as it is,' he added, shooting a glance at Og-Grim-Dog.

'Rather unnecessary,' Dog muttered.

'We're in the industrial sector,' Little El told them as he led them out of the yard and onto what had to be a main street. It was wide and well maintained, surfaced with stone. 'The palace is some way off.'

'You have Discount Dungeon Supplies in Kuthenia?' Og asked him, indicating a branch of the store on the opposite side of the road. The signage proclaimed it as a superstore, and indeed, it was the largest shop Grim had ever seen.

'A new addition to the capital,' Little El revealed. 'Rumour is that they are now the main supplier to the Imperial Army.'

It was the middle of the night and barely a light could be seen in the city. Sometimes they heard voices, but the streets seemed empty. If street thugs did peer at them from the shadows as they passed, they elected to let them go on their way and wait for a softer target. They walked by people's homes and through squares. Canals crisscrossed the city, creating straight lines wherever they went and requiring their party to cross the many bridges that spanned them. They made their way from the edge of Pengshui into its heart, where, finally, they came upon the Imperial Palace.

It wasn't what Grim had been expecting. He had envisaged it tall and grand, like Fell Towers. Instead, this was long, wide and grand. The palace was a complex of buildings enclosed within a rectangular walled area. There were enough lights inside the palace for him to make out the peaked roofs of several buildings beyond the walls, but none were especially tall. The wall stretched out in a straight line before them, disappearing into darkness. In front of it, Grim could just make out the shimmer of water.

'How do we cross the canal?' he asked.

'There are many crossing points into the palace,' Little El replied. 'Come, I will show you the one to use.'

He took them off to the left, staying parallel with the palace wall. They moved warily now, aware that there would likely be guards on the walls, even though they couldn't see any sign of them.

Little El stopped them opposite a bridge. It crossed the canal and led to a gate in the wall.

'Through that gate, to the left,' he said, pointing to the location he described, 'there are half a dozen slave huts. One of them will have a green light on.'

'A green light?' Og asked.

'A candle, inside a green lantern,' the barbarian explained. 'That is Ericka's hut. She has agreed to take you to the home of the Emperor and his family. But let me make it clear. There are hundreds of soldiers in the palace. If you're seen, you're dead. Or worse, they take you alive.'

'That's all very well,' said Gurin, 'but how are we going to get past these walls without being seen?'

'Well,' said Simba, 'it doesn't seem like such a hard thing to do. We just need to eliminate any guards in this section of the wall.'

'But we need to get in first, before we can start eliminating people.'

'Oh. No problem. Wait here until I open the gate,' Simba said, setting off.

Assata caught the dark elf by the arm. 'And if you fail?'

'Then assume I'm dead or captured and call off the mission.'

THE IMPERIAL PALACE

After all the waiting they had done, Grim assumed there would be a lot more of it to come. He was surprised, therefore, to see the gate slowly swing open not long after Simba had disappeared over the wall.

'There's our cue,' Gurin muttered, wincing as he got to his feet.

'Good luck,' said Little El.

Assata clasped his hand. Then their barbarian guide disappeared into the shadows, and the three companions made their way to the palace.

They began to cross the bridge, Grim looking warily up at the wall, in case it was a trap. But as they neared the gate, he made out the white-haired figure of the dark elf, gesturing for them to hurry.

They set foot inside the palace walls and Simba closed the gate behind them.

'This way,' he whispered, pointing.

About forty feet inside the perimeter of the walls was a cluster of huts, and a green light flickered outside one of them.

'The guards?' Assata asked Simba.

'Five of them altogether. I've dumped their bodies out of sight. But for all we know, there could be a change soon. We don't have time to waste.'

They made their way towards the hut, Grim doing his very best to go quietly. He was helped a little by the well-manicured grass underfoot. But they can't have been silent, because the door to the hut opened as they approached, and a small figure ushered them inside.

Slaves of all ages were sleeping on the floor, while a few had been woken by the goings on and were staring at the arrivals to their hut. The woman, carrying the green lantern with her, followed them inside and closed the door. She was small, much older than Assata. To Grim's eyes, she was incredibly delicate looking, and yet there was a look of determination in her eyes.

'Ericka?' Assata asked.

'Yes.'

'I am Assata.' She pulled her sleeve up to show the woman her tattoo. 'You know why we are here?'

'I do. Do you need anything?'

'No. We are ready when you are.'

'The guards?'

'Taken care of,' said Simba.

'Then let's go. It's not fair to keep you here. I am comfortable with risking my own life, but not those of my family.'

With that, Ericka led them back outside. They followed her across the lawn and onto a path that took them towards a group of larger buildings in the palace, all with upturned eaves.

'I work in the Inner Court,' she whispered. She glanced at their blank looks. 'Where the imperial family lives,' she added.

They cut past extravagant looking wooden buildings, coloured red and orange and green, with yellow roof tiles. Many had steps leading up to their entrances. But Ericka kept them to the shadows, without comment, until she raised a hand and stopped them.

'See there,' she said, pointing ahead of them. 'That is the Inner Court.'

The Inner Court was raised significantly higher than the rest of the palace. Grim could see more buildings like the ones they had passed. He could see a wide set of stairs that led up to the Court. And, of course, he could see guards, both at the foot and at the top of the stairs.

'I can go no farther,' Ericka whispered. 'If you walk in a straight line from the top of the stairs you will come to a large building, the Hall of Supremacy. It is coloured bright red, with golden statues on the roof. You cannot miss it. The princess has her room on the top floor, second from the left. No men are allowed in her room, only female attendants. Please try not to harm the attendants.'

'Any ideas how to get past these guards?' Gurin asked her.

'Sorry. I have done what I promised to do. Long live the Resistance.'

Ericka clasped hands with Assata and then left them, retreating the way they had come.

'Well, that's useful, isn't it?' said Gurin sarcastically. 'Now what do we do?'

They looked at one another and then back to the heavily guarded approach to the Inner Court. No-one seemed to have an answer. Until Assata turned to Og-Grim-Dog.

'I think we're going to need a distraction.'

*

The truth was, Og-Grim-Dog were quite content to play the role Assata wanted. They just weren't suited for subtlety or stealth. This was a much closer match to their skill set.

They charged at the guards stationed at the foot of the steps, coming out of the night like a creature from your worst nightmare. It helped that their ogre eyes were better in the dark than humans were—they could see their enemy a fraction quicker. When the Kuthenians did lock eyes with the ogre, their brains froze, or panicked: unable to interpret what exactly it was that came roaring at them. Og's pike lashed out, the range he had longer than anything they had ever experienced, the wicked blade at the end coming at them before it could be expected. Grim carried on into them, allowing Dog to swing about with his mace, barking with pleasure.

It didn't take them long to turn the soldiers into a bloody mess on the steps. But now the element of surprise had gone, and soldiers began to emerge from around the palace. They came down the steps in a row, spears and shields at the ready. More came from the buildings in the Inner Court, and from the buildings behind them. They shouted to one another—insects, working together to bring down the beast.

Grim hadn't caught a glimpse of his three companions. That was good. If he had seen nothing, the chances were high that they had slipped by the Kuthenians unseen also.

'I don't think fighting our way up these steps is the best idea,' Grim said.

'Agreed,' said Og.

'Well, there's plenty of people to kill down here,' said Dog magnanimously.

Grim backed away from the row of spears preparing to skewer them. Suddenly, he turned and ran in the opposite direction. Here, the Kuthenian soldiers had yet to organise themselves into anything resembling a formation, simply running towards the sound of fighting. They were unprepared for what came their way. Those with the presence of mind, turned and ran. Those who hesitated were battered by a mace, a huge blunt weapon swung with the force only an ogre could muster. Any who took a direct hit didn't get back up again.

The move bought them some time, but the row of spears had now reached the bottom of the steps, and more soldiers had joined it. Still more came from every conceivable direction, perhaps a hundred now on the scene.

Grim had to act quickly.

He barged his way up the steps of one of the buildings, kicking open the wooden doors.

'We might be getting ourselves into a situation we can't escape from,' Og warned him in one ear, as Grim marched into what looked like a temple.

But outnumbered as they were, Grim knew they wouldn't last long in the open. Even if they were run down inside this temple—killed or captured—they were buying their friends the precious time they needed.

The interior of the temple seemed empty, but it was dark, and there were many places for enemies to lurk undetected. Grim decided to make for a set of stairs that led up to the top floor. As he began the climb, the doors he had come through swung back open. Hesitantly at first, then with more confidence, the Kuthenian soldiers entered the temple. As the numbers increased, they began to march towards the ogre's position on the stairs.

'At least we have the height advantage here,' Grim said.

It was part statement, part question. Were his brothers happy for him to make a stand here?

'We can't hold them back forever,' said Dog dubiously. He was more of a close-quarters fighter.

'Looks like we have a problem,' said Og.

Looking down at the enemy, Grim saw several bow staves being pulled back. They had to move. But it was too late, as the twang of the bows signalled several arrows were flying in their direction. Og tried to block the missiles, but he was hit in the arm and let out a bellow of pain.

Grim acted quickly now, turning around and climbing the rest of the stairs. He didn't stop.

'Get ready!' he shouted and ran headlong into the exterior wall.

Grim's thinking was that the thin-looking wooden walls of the temple would give way from the force of a large ogre throwing their weight at it. Fortunately, he was right. The wall exploded outwards in a shower of broken wood and masonry and Og-Grim-Dog found themselves falling down to the ground below. It wasn't a pleasant landing, though Grim had given his brother's enough warning for them to release their weapons mid-fall and use their arms to help cushion the impact. They were fortunate again, that they landed on grass.

Og-Grim-Dog picked themselves up. The first job was to retrieve their weapons. Og gasped in pain as he gripped his pike, a broken arrow still protruding from his arm.

Grim knew that more arrows would come for them if they didn't move. He ran away from the temple and the other buildings, across the palace lawn, in the hope that the darkness might conceal them. It didn't, entirely.

'Hey!' a familiar voice hissed at them from the darkness.

Grim stopped, turning in the direction where he thought the sound had come from. Gurin was running towards them, axe held in both hands. Then, not far behind him, was Assata. She carried an inert body over one shoulder.

'Keep moving!'

Gurin ran past them, and Grim ran after him.

'Is that the princess?' Dog asked Assata as she drew level with them.

'Yes.'

'What about Simba?'

'He's holding them up for a while.'

'Let me carry her.'

Assata stopped, and Dog put his mace in his belt. The princess was transferred from one to the other, and the barbarian drew her sword. In the time it took to accomplish this, Simba caught up to them. He held a bloody sword in each hand, but they barely seemed to slow his swift pace.

Wordlessly, the three of them chased after Gurin. Grim did his best to keep up, but his lungs began to fail him. It was all very well for Dog to carry the princess—it was no problem for him. But it meant extra weight for Grim, and running had never been a strength.

It was only when they ran past Ericka's hut that Grim realised where they were. The walls of the palace came into view ahead.

Please let the gate be open and undefended, he prayed silently to Lord Vyana.

Grim was of the belief that the fact that the gate happened to be open and undefended wasn't simply because he had prayed to Vyana. The world was a bit more complicated than that. Still, he gave Him his thanks anyway, and thanked His Horde of Winged Hyenas as well.

Gurin was waiting for them, his chest heaving as he caught his breath. With a nod, he turned and led them into the city. The dwarf had a way with directions, and he had Assata to help him. Grim was confident that they would get them back to the tunnel under the walls of Pengshui. All he had to do was concentrate on putting one foot in front of the other, as quickly as he could.

PRINCESS BORTE

I didn't think you'd do it,' Little El admitted, his eyes popping out of his head at the sight of the princess of the Kuthenian Empire laid out cold in his warehouse.

'There's not much time,' Assata stressed once more.

Adrenaline was still coursing through their bodies and it felt like the Resistance man was moving in slow motion.

'Right. Sorry. Well, our stores are lost, there's no point in trying to save them. They'll discover the tunnel,' he added.

Grim could see the man's mind ticking over, making decisions in a panic that he should have made earlier, if only he hadn't completely discounted their chances of success.

'I'll come with you,' he decided. 'Lead you out and hand you over to someone who can get you far from the city. I'll give the order to keep the Kuthenians away from here for as long as possible—give us a head start.'

Grim let the others take the tunnel first, Assata and Gurin carrying the princess between them. If he and his brothers got stuck in there, at least they wouldn't be trapping anyone else with them.

It was hard work, pushing their exhausted body through the tight squeeze of a tunnel. Grim's leg muscles began to cramp, over-worked and in need of rest. Og still used his hand to help them crawl through, but he had gone silent now, and Grim knew from experience that wasn't a good sign. They'd had no time to treat the arrow wound and part of the shaft still stuck out of his brother's arm, no doubt scraping along the wall every time they got stuck.

Finally, they made it out, relieved to find their friends waiting for them and not a troop of Kuthenian soldiers. They lay down on their back, Grim stretching out his legs. Gurin passed them and returned to the tunnel.

'What's he doing?' Dog demanded.

'Collapsing the tunnel,' Simba replied.

The sound of an axe striking the wooden supports echoed back down the tunnel.

'Does he need some help?' asked Dog.

I wish you would stop offering our help all the time, Grim said to himself, though he had been very close to saying it out loud.

'I think if there's one thing dwarves can do by themselves,' Simba replied, 'it's collapse a tunnel. And I'm really not sure there's room in there for you to swing your mace about.'

Sure enough, the sound of cracking wood and tumbling earth could be heard, quickly followed by a blast of dust and an axe-wielding dwarf exiting the tunnel.

Little El gave a sigh of relief. 'That should buy us some time. They've got to find the tunnel first, then discover it's been collapsed. Then they'll need to work out that it comes out here. Meanwhile, I'll have taken you to a nearby resistance cell and you'll be on your way.'

'Getting a wagon would be useful,' said Assata, looking at the prone figure of the princess laid out on the floor. 'And finding someone who can treat wounds,' she added, her gaze moving to Og's arm.

✻

The wagon trundled through the Kuthenian countryside. Outside, Simba took his turn driving the horses. Inside, there was the most impressive collection of glares and glowers Grim had ever seen. Gurin Fuckaxe wore his default expression, which was a mightily miserable grimace. Og, his arm finally bandaged up, was in too much pain to sleep, leaving him in a foul mood. Assata stared daggers at their captive, her fingers twitching, as if—left to their own accord—they would grab the girl's neck and not let go. But the blackest looks of all, Grim was surprised to note, came from Princess Borte herself.

Unconscious, Borte had been agreeable company. Petite, with long black hair, she had not looked much different to a human child to Grim's eyes, and he had developed some sympathy towards her, abducted from her home in the dead of night. Conscious, she had a bit more to say for herself.

'So, let me get this right,' she said, her voice dripping with contempt. 'Kidnapping me and taking me to the Dark Lord is somehow going to be a victory for the slaves of the Empire?'

'A war with the Dark Lord will hasten the demise of your evil empire and the emancipation of my people,' Assata retorted.

'Your people aren't going to be helped by some hapless slave rebellion,' said Borte. 'That will just result in their massacre. Who has the money and the weapons, you fool? The end of slavery will come when the Emperor is persuaded of its merit. And it so happens, I was making good progress on that front. Those attendants in my room you threatened to skewer with your sword were slaves I had freed. What will my father and the other leading men of the Empire do when they find out that the Resistance was behind this? Start treating their slaves better? If you had any sense at all, you would end this idiocy and release me.'

Assata laughed, though there was no humour in it. 'We'll be waiting forever if we sit and wait for the Kuthenians to end their evil institution. Slavery will end with the blood of innocents, the same way it was born. You think your father indulging you, by freeing a few house slaves, is the start of something more? You're naïve to the world, princess, and naïve to think you can persuade me to release you.'

Borte rolled her eyes. 'And as for you,' she said, turning her attention to Og-Grim-Dog and Gurin. 'You've kidnapped me because the Dark Lord ordered you to? If he wants a war so bad, why doesn't he send an army to Kuthenia, instead of an ogre and a dwarf? Does he even have an army?'

Grim recalled their failed attempts to train the menials. *Not much of one,* he admitted to himself.

'I'm afraid he's dropped you in it. My father's generals won't be forgiving when they catch up to us.'

'It's not just a war he wants,' Gurin murmured in response. 'It's the throne. He intends to marry you when we bring you to him.'

That piece of news held her tongue for a while. She stared at them then, a mixture of incredulity and apprehension on her face. Grim felt more than a little embarrassed and had to look away.

'You think you can cross half the Kuthenian Empire with me, and not get caught?' she asked finally, rallying. 'The Imperial Army will catch up to us in a day or two, if not hours. And I won't be sorry to see you get justice when they do.'

But for all Princess Borte's confidence, the days went by and there was no sign of any chasing soldiers. They left the wagon behind, walking from one settlement to the next during the night, aided by the Resistance. As each day passed, Borte got a little bit quieter. For whatever reason, the Emperor's forces didn't come.

The days turned into weeks and when they crossed the Kuthenian border, it was without incident. Borte didn't say a word.

GOOD NEWS AND BAD NEWS

By the time the tall, finger-like spires of Fell Towers came into view, winter had long past given up its hold over Gal'azu—even of this remote spot. Colour had appeared in the hills and the woods and the meadows, where there had been none before.

On their approach to the tall gates of the stronghold, Grim could see there had been other changes. Sheev's had grown—it had outdoor seating now, currently full of menials. In addition, a new building had been erected next door. Grim read the signage—Discount Dungeon Supplies: Depot.

He saw Assata and Gurin looking in the same direction with interest, no doubt enticed by the thought of browsing the weapon racks. But they had business with the Dark Lord first.

A helmeted figure appeared above them. 'Password?' it shouted down.

'Heinous,' Simba shouted up.

'That hasn't been the password for some time,' the menial responded doubtfully.

'We've been away on the Dark Lord's business for months,' Simba responded. 'We've just got back.'

Two more menials emerged, and a conversation ensued, not loud enough to carry down to the five figures waiting down below.

'They're going to refuse us entry,' said Grim, excited at the prospect of progress in the menials' ability to guard Fell Towers.

'I'll wager they don't,' said Dog.

'Alright then. Give us a moment,' came a voice.

The gates to Fell Towers swung open.

✶

The Dark Lord was in his element.

'You have done well, henchmen,' he said grandiosely, once they had recounted their adventures in Kuthenia. 'The Kuthenian Empire has taken a blow to its very heart, in a place where they felt most safe. And soon I will deliver a second blow,' he added, striding forwards to where Princess Borte had been told to kneel, her hands bound. He took her chin between his thumb and forefinger. 'For soon I will marry this beauty and lay claim to the Jade Throne for myself.'

'You will not,' said Borte, wrenching her head backwards. 'Because marriage requires consent, and I would never consent to marry a halfwit like you in a thousand years.'

'Oh, she's a hot-headed little minx, isn't she?' said the Dark Lord with glee, looking about the throne room. 'It makes me want to have the ceremony immediately!'

'Great, the sooner I can cut your throat while you sleep,' said Borte.

'But no,' he said, ignoring the comment. 'I can wait for my pleasure. The wedding will take place a month from now. I want it to be the grandest occasion Fell Towers has ever seen!'

Behind the Dark Lord, at her place by his throne, Lilith cleared her throat. She kept her face neutral, but Grim could still detect an air of disapproval.

'My Lord, perhaps it would be wiser not to wait a full month for the ceremony? Surely that will hold back our plans, and give our enemies more time to attempt a rescue? Once the marriage is done, and you impregnate Her Royal Highness, her value to the Emperor will diminish and Kuthenia will be more likely to accept a fait accompli.'

Princess Borte made an unpleasant barfing sound.

'Pah, what do I care? I *want* this war with Kuthenia, remember? And I want my wedding to the Dark Lady to be perfect, too. I am decided on it. Wro'Kuburni'-Dy-Hrath'Simbowa, please escort my future wife to the basement, where I have a cell prepared for her.'

Not unkindly, Simba pulled the princess to her feet, and led her away. Grim looked away as they passed, unable to shake off a sense of shame over her predicament.

The Dark Lord watched her go. It was impossible to tell for sure what kind of expression he had under his helmet, but Grim was pretty sure it was a smile.

'Right. Any other business?' he asked his adviser.

'The barbarian woman. Assata,' Lilith reminded him.

'Of course, yes. Now, you played a very important role in bringing me my Dark Lady and have proven your worth. I would like to offer you a job as henchman. Is that right?' he asked, turning back to Lilith. 'Or should it be henchwoman?'

'Henchman is fine.'

'Wonderful.' He turned back to Assata. 'I understand it's not everybody's thing, so feel free to think about it. Even if you don't take us up on the offer, please stay until the wedding. It would be lovely for you to be there, since you played such an important role in bringing us together.'

'I don't think being a henchman is really my thing,' said Assata. 'I did what I did for my people. But I think I would like to stay for the wedding. See it through to the end, if you will.'

'Of course. I understand. I only want people here at Fell Towers who want to be here. And who knows, we might just change your mind while you stay with us. Now, any questions?'

'I've got one,' said Og. 'Why is there a Discount Dungeon Supplies depot here?'

Lilith gave an annoyed sigh but let her master field the question.

'We've decided to close down the weapons manufactory,' said the Dark Lord. 'Free up the workforce there. DDS are supplying all our military needs now.'

'Sheev's has got bigger since we left,' Dog noted.

'Yes. We made a tough decision there, too. Sheev's supplies all our food now. The refectory has closed down too.'

First Grim heard the intake of breath, then Dog's tormented howl.

'Nooooo!'

✻

After such a long time away from Fell Towers, all Og-Grim-Dog wanted to do was sit in their room in the basement and do nothing. Still in mourning over the loss of the refectory, they would venture out to Sheev's a few times a day for their meals, and this went some way to ease the grief. Dog would stare into the distance, a tear in one eye, shoving fries into his mouth, until Grim would ask whether he might have some of *his* meal. Often, Dog was too upset to feed Grim, and Og would have to do it all.

After a few days, this routine was broken when Gurin came down to the basement to fetch them.

'We're all wanted in the throne room,' the dwarf said unenthusiastically.

'What for?' Og asked.

Gurin just shrugged, and so they got to Grim's feet and followed the dwarf up the stone steps to the next level of the keep. Entering the throne room, it seemed that everyone else was ready and waiting for them. Menials lined the walls of the rectangular room, while Assata and Simba stood before the Dark Lord on his throne. Grim got the impression that the Dark Lord enjoyed these audiences. Lilith, stood as ever to one side of the throne, gave the opposite impression.

'Ah!' said the Dark Lord as they approached. 'We're all here. Now, do you want to hear the good news or the bad news?'

'The good news,' said Dog in a nervous voice, as if he couldn't take any more disappointment.

'The good news comes from Kuthenia. Our spies tell us that you didn't just capture the princess. You killed the emperor, too! Why didn't you tell me?'

Grim shared a confused look with the others. 'What happened in the Hall of Supremacy?' he asked.

'The three of us never left each other's side,' said Assata with a frown. 'We went to Borte's apartments. Simba subdued her with some kind of neck pinch. I kept her attendants quiet. Gurin was on lookout. None of us went to the emperor's apartments.'

'Then *you* must have killed the emperor, ogre?' the Dark Lord asked.

'Yes!' said Dog.

The Dark Lord clapped in pleasure. Everyone else stared at Dog sceptically—Lilith's dark eyes bored into his remorselessly.

'Well, that is, we killed a number of Kuthenians while we were making our distraction,' he clarified. 'The emperor could have been one of them.'

'Could have been,' the Dark Lord agreed, though he sounded doubtful. 'I suppose it doesn't really matter who did it. The fact is, he's dead. When I marry his daughter, my claim to the throne will be hard to deny.'

'What about the bad news?' Gurin asked, sounding less than impressed with the good news.

'Well, your work in Kuthenia has drawn attention our way. Our eyes in Mer Khazer have sent us news.'

Grim shared a look with his brothers. They knew it was Brother Kane whom the Dark Lord spoke of.

'The Bureau of Dungeoneering have added Fell Towers to their list of dungeons. The heroes of the Bureau now have the right to come here, rescue my soon to be wife and loot my treasures.'

'Will they come?' Simba asked, knowing full well the previous careers of his associates. 'Surely they wouldn't dare.'

'They'll come,' Gurin said. 'Quality loot is thin on the ground these days. Throw in the chance to rescue a kidnapped princess, and it will be hard to resist for some adventurers, whatever the risks.'

'Then we need to prepare,' said Lilith. 'If an invading army from Kuthenia is now less likely, we need to think about how we stop a break-in by the Bureau. Gurin, you were a member of the Bureau for years. Please take the lead on this.'

Gurin nodded his agreement.

'Any other questions?' asked the Dark Lord.

Lilith turned her gaze to Og-Grim-Dog.

'Please, don't,' Grim whispered to his brothers under his breath. He really didn't think bringing up the refectory again would help.

'Very well,' the Dark Lord said into the silence. 'You are dismissed.'

Assata closed the doors of the throne room behind them. 'Well?' she said.

'I suppose I should look into the defences of this place,' said Gurin.

'Why not take Simba with you?' Assata suggested. 'Presumably he knows this place better than the rest of us.'

'What about you?' Gurin asked.

'Someone needs to tell Princess Borte about the emperor. It's not a pleasant job, but I'd rather she heard it from my lips than the Dark Lord's. It's her father, after all. Will you come with me, Og-Grim-Dog?'

Put on the spot, Grim desperately began to think of an excuse to avoid going with the barbarian.

'It's the least we should do,' said Og.

'Very well,' said Gurin, looking relieved to have avoided that task. He and Simba left them to it.

'Let's get this done now,' Assata said. 'Lead on, I haven't visited the basement yet.'

Reluctantly, Grim led the barbarian to the trapdoor that led down to the lower level of the keep. The menials on duty, now used to the coming and going of the ogre, raised the door and let them pass down into the musty depths. Descending to the bottom, Dog pointed to one corner.

'Do you want to see our room?' he asked Assata, in a childish attempt to forestall their meeting with the princess.

'Maybe later,' said the barbarian curtly, and Grim carried on until they were looking through the bars at Princess Borte. Her cell was large and comfortable looking from Grim's perspective, with rugs and cushions and other luxuries. Half a dozen lanterns did a reasonable job of keeping the gloom of the basement at bay. Compared to her rooms in the Imperial Palace, however, Grim suspected it was a bit of a disappointment.

She raised her head blearily, as if she had been asleep. It was hard to keep track of day and night underground.

'Come to gloat?' she asked them.

'No,' said Assata. 'You may not believe me, but I take no pleasure in seeing you here. I have come with bad news, as soon as I heard it.'

'Bad news?' asked Borte, gesturing to her prison cell. 'Is that meant to be a joke?'

'There's no easy way to say this,' said Assata. 'The Dark Lord has informed us that your father, the emperor, is dead.'

'What?' said the princess, one word conveying a score of emotions, from suspicion to despair. 'How?'

'We're not sure. The report he has says that we killed him, but that cannot be. Was he ill or frail?'

'No. What else was said?'

'Nothing. I'm sorry.'

'You have our condolences,' said Og.

'I don't want your condolences, monster!' Borte suddenly screamed. 'I want out of this nightmare! I have to get back home, do you understand? Kuthenia needs me. The people need me.' She looked at Assata. 'Free and slave alike.' She screwed her face up then. 'This is exactly what you wanted, isn't it? A civil war, thousands of innocents killed, children orphaned and starving. I'm surprised you can hold back your sadistic grin.'

'I won't be a hypocrite and pretend I didn't wish harm on Kuthenia. This is the best chance my people have of freedom. But nonetheless I am sorry for your loss. I know the pain of losing a good parent.'

'Get lost, the pair of you! I can't stomach the commiserations of people who caused all of this.'

'Come,' said Assata, and they left Borte with her grief. 'Now, you mentioned that there are others down here?' she said after they put some distance between themselves and Borte's cell.

'There are two others,' said Dog. 'The Dark Lord's pet. And his brother.'

'Of course,' said Assata. 'Because it wasn't weird enough down here already. Why don't you show me?'

'What the hell do you want?' Fraser demanded, his eyes screwed up from days of darkness. He hadn't been afforded the luxury of light in his cell like Borte had. 'Is that you Jonty, you wazzock!'

'Jonty?' Assata asked.

'That's the Dark Lord's name apparently,' said Og.

'My name is Assata. I'm a guest here. Why does your brother keep you in here?' Assata asked Fraser.

'Because he's madder than a bucket of wolpertingers, that's why.'

'Oh, I'm sorry. Can we get you anything?'

'Drink and food. And a change of clothes.'

Assata looked at Og-Grim-Dog. 'Maybe you could look after him since you live down here? See to his basic needs?'

Grim thought he had never felt so ashamed before.

'Of course,' said Og, sounding equally miserable.

A WARNING

Over the next few days, preparations for the wedding between the Dark Lord and Princess Borte got in full swing. Gurin, the new head of security, recruited extra menials for guard duty. But that still left hundreds spare, who would previously have been making weapons or food, tasks now subcontracted out to DDS and Sheev's. They were put to work decorating Fell Towers for the festivities. The old refectory was transformed into a grand reception room for the guests of the happy couple. Sheev's produced special limited-edition figurines of the Dark Lord and Princess Borte, which began to appear with their meals, and were highly sought after by the loyal menials.

With two weeks to go until the wedding date, an atmosphere of excitement and anticipation had spread around most parts of Fell Towers. Grim had to admit that the atmosphere hadn't permeated down to the basement. The Dark Lord's brother, pet and future wife remained a little glum.

Lilith called the henchmen to a meeting in her office on the top floor of the keep. Assata, still not persuaded to join the Dark Lord's service, wasn't there.

'I have received a warning about the arrival of a party of heroes from the Bureau of Dungeoneering. They could get here any day now.'

'Do we know who sent the warning?' Og asked pointedly.

Lilith took a moment to study the three of them. Grim knew she was thinking, but her dark eyes were impossible to read. Then she made up her mind.

'I'm going to trust you,' she said, 'but this information is to be shared with no-one else. I mean no-one. Understand?' When she received their assent, the Dark Lord's adviser continued. 'Brother Kane is a henchman of the Dark Lord. He is with them.'

Grim saw Gurin's eyes widen in surprise, but he said nothing.

'Obviously,' Lilith continued, 'they have no idea about his real allegiance, so that gives us an advantage. But that doesn't mean we should underestimate the threat they pose.'

'Who's with him?' Gurin asked.

Gurin's question sparked a sudden fear in Grim, something he hadn't even considered until now. *What if their friends were in this party?*

'I don't have names,' said Lilith, 'but he told me there are four others with him. A knight, thief, ranger and enchantress.'

Grim let out a sigh of relief. None of those descriptions matched any of the friends they had made in Mer Khazer.

'It is the enchantress I am most concerned about,' Lilith said. 'We must be on our guard.'

*

Og-Grim-Dog awoke to the sounds of shouts and crashes coming from above. There was no doubt about it. A battle raged upstairs.

'Sounds like it's time to fight,' said Dog, making a poor attempt to sound disappointed.

Grim went to the corner of their little room, where his brothers grabbed their weapons: pike and mace. That was all they needed to get ready.

They left their room and went to the stone steps that led up to the next level of the keep. There they waited, listening.

'You're in trouble now,' Borte's voice drifted to them from her cell. 'The Kuthenians are here.'

'I don't think so, Your Highness,' said Og gently.

'What?' barked Dog, his voice animated and loud. 'You think it's the trespassers from the Bureau? There's a full-scale skirmish going on up there!'

'I hear no Kuthenian accents,' Og said. 'Mainly menials.'

'Then who are the menials fighting?' Dog demanded. Grim's brother sounded ready to explode in his eagerness for a fight. 'I think we'll have to go up there and investigate.'

'Gurin said we should stay down here,' Grim reminded him, 'and guard the princess.'

'Yes, but there's something strange going on up there. We can't just leave them to it.'

'Please don't stay on my account,' Borte's voice drifted over again.

'What do you think, Og?' Grim asked.

'Maybe we should have a look.'

'Yes!' Dog cried in exultation.

With an uneasy feeling, Grim began to ascend the stone steps. He really wasn't sure about this course of action. What if, by opening the trapdoor, they revealed the location of the princess to the enemy? Then again, they had friends up there that might need their help. As they approached the top of the steps, he heard the crack of weapons striking metal armour and wooden shields, the shouts and screams of menials.

Og and Dog flung open the trapdoor and Grim quickly ran up the final steps. Only then did he look around to get his bearings. Menials were fighting against menials, and at first sight he could make no sense of it. Then he realised that one group had forced their way into the keep, and amongst this band of menials was a human. She was easy to spot. Wearing a deep blue dress and cloak, she held aloft a staff with a glowing, pale blue orb on the end of it. Her mouth moved as if she were talking, but amongst the cacophony of the battle Grim could make out no words. Whatever she was saying, the menials about her were doing her bidding.

The enchantress, Grim realised. *She has charmed the feeble-minded menials to do her bidding.*

Opposing this invasion of the keep were Gurin, Simba, Assata and Lilith, with a second group of menials. Amongst both groups of menials were archers, whose arrows sailed tragically wide of each other. Lilith screamed at the underlings with her to ignore the enchantment, while the other three were attempting to cut a path through the charmed menials, no doubt with the aim of striking down the witch who controlled them.

'Og-Grim-Dog?' Assata shouted over, noticing their sudden arrival.

Gurin turned to look. ''Bout time. Give us a hand, will you?' he said sourly.

'Wait!' Lilith shouted, her voice louder than Grim thought possible, stopping him in his tracks. 'Kane and the others! I thought they would be attempting to rescue the princess?'

'No,' said Dog. 'We've seen no sign of 'em.'

Grim wondered about that. Clearly, Brother Kane and the other members of his party had separated from the enchantress. But if they hadn't gone to the basement to rescue Borte, where were they? Then a thought struck him.

'The crystal sword!' he exclaimed.

Lilith's eyes widened. The Dark Lord had shown them the room containing the weapon he called his bane. The one thing that could kill him. What if the adventurers had decided to kill the Dark Lord first, *then* free the princess? It was bold, but the more Grim thought about it, the more it sounded like a rather clever plan.

'Stop them!' Lilith shouted. 'All of you! I will hold the enchantress off here until you are done. Be quick, your master is in danger!'

Wasting no time, Assata and the others disengaged from the turned menials. Grim ran ahead to the stairs that led up to the top floor of the keep. It was possible that Gurin and Simba knew of the room that the Dark Lord had shown to Grim and his brothers—a wooden stand in an otherwise empty room, with a crystal sword atop it. But maybe he hadn't, in which case Og-Grim-Dog were the only ones who knew where it was.

He ran up the stairs, heard the welcoming sounds of the others pounding behind him. Then Simba was somehow ahead, the swift-footed dark elf gaining the top of the stairs and heading for the corridor.

Well, he's definitely been shown the room, Grim decided.

He followed Simba into the expensively furnished corridor, his lungs bursting, Assata and Gurin with him now. The far end of the corridor was red with the blood of the two dead menials whose job had been to guard the door. The dark elf ignored the sight, making for the open door to the room. The door that the Dark Lord kept locked; the lock that only the Dark Lord had a key for.

Suddenly, a figure appeared in the doorway. Encased in metal from head to foot, it was already launching a gauntleted fist at the dark elf. For all his speed, it was too late for Simba to stop or change direction. The punch landed with a dull thud and the dark elf slumped to the floor, unmoving. Through the thin slot of his visor, the knight looked past Simba to the three-headed ogre coming down the corridor—Dog barking out a challenge—and shut the door.

THE DARK LORD'S BANE

Grim didn't stop, running at the door and twisting at the last moment, so that his hip and Dog's shoulder slammed into it. The door gave way and he stumbled into the room. Og's shoulder guard was struck heavily by a weapon and Grim found himself tottering over, unable to get his feet under him. He crashed into the wooden stand in the centre of the room and fell to the floor.

Og managed to get the palm of his hand onto the floor and push up, allowing Grim to get to his feet. He sensed figures moving around him. As his brothers re-armed, he focused on two combats: Assata fought against the armoured knight, trading blows against his sword and shield; while Gurin fended off a short spear wielded by a lanky human, who was likely the ranger Brother Kane had mentioned. The man's reach was much longer than the dwarf's, and Gurin was being forced backwards to the far wall.

Grim took a step forward to intervene, when Dog let out a warning bark. Spinning around, he saw a small human form darting away from Dog's mace. The thief, Grim supposed—no doubt he had pick-locked their way into the room. In both hands he gripped a crystal sword. The Dark Lord's bane.

In the corner of the room there was a fourth intruder. The cowl of his cloak covered his face, but Grim recognised him, nonetheless. Brother Kane.

A thud sounded behind them and this time Og shouted out a warning. Grim turned to see Assata sprawled on the floor. By the looks of it, she'd taken a blow from the metal clad knight's shield rather than his sword. Og lashed out with his pike. The knight's smooth mail deflected the blow, but at least it diverted the warrior's attention to them, and away from the prone barbarian.

Grim knew they were in trouble. His allies had rapidly been taken out of the fight and he and his brothers would struggle if outnumbered.

The knight came at them, his shield pushing aside Og's pike. He side-stepped Dog's swinging mace and then his sword twisted in, Grim unable to avoid it as it pierced his chest mail and sank into muscle. Grim retreated, pulling free of the sword, though his back muscles tensed in anticipation of the crystal sword stabbing in from behind.

Instead, the sound of a struggle could be heard. Risking a glance, he saw that Brother Kane had one arm around the thief's neck. In his opposite hand the cleric held a thin dagger—the thief's grip about his wrist preventing him from using it. The man's other hand was trying to wrench free of Brother Kane's hold on him. The crystal sword now lay on the floor.

It seemed that everyone noticed the sword at the same time. A rush of bodies converged on the space, the adventurers from the Bureau desperate to regain the weapon, the Dark Lord's servants equally desperate to prevent them.

The knight came for Og-Grim-Dog again. This time, Og used his pike as a defensive staff, keeping him at arm's length. The knight's sword-strike was met by Dog's mace. Ordinarily, a blow from that mace would break an arm. The knight's armour no doubt absorbed some of the damage, but still he lost his grip on his sword, his visored helmet watching it sail across the room, out of reach.

But just as Grim took a step towards his opponent, thinking he had the upper hand, an almighty force slammed him away. He wobbled, somehow staying on his feet, as he spied a spear protruding from Og's shoulder. His brother dropped his pike, then cried out in agony as Dog ripped the spear out.

Grim looked up to see their assailant. The ranger held the crystal sword. Behind him, Gurin was sat against the wall, face pale, his hands clutched about his belly where dark red blood pumped from a wound. Nearby, Brother Kane cowered on the floor beside the thief's body, whose head was almost completely detached from his shoulders.

'Go!' the ranger shouted, and he and the knight ran for the exit to the room.

'After them!' said Brother Kane. 'I'll tend to the fallen.'

Grim chased after the two adventurers. The knight was already in the corridor. Behind him, the ranger found his legs taken from him as Assata kicked out from her position on the floor. Moving too fast to right himself, the ranger went down, the crystal sword leaving his grip and skittering across the floor. Turning at the noise, the knight reached down to grab the sword. For a moment he looked at Og-Grim-Dog bearing down on them and obviously decided his friend was lost, because he turned back to the corridor and ran.

Dog's mace came down on the ranger's head as Grim ran past. There was only the knight left, now. But he held the weapon that could kill the Dark Lord, and despite his heavy armour, and for all Grim tried, the knight was faster, too. Og's spear wound was stealing his stamina—his breathing heavy now, and his legs aquiver.

The knight stopped at a door along the corridor. Barging it open, he charged inside.

Following behind, Grim felt a shiver of apprehension. He had no idea where the Dark Lord was—but the knight seemed to. Grim reached the door and entered the room.

It looked like he was too late. The Dark Lord faced the knight—his own, dark metallic sword against the rose-coloured crystal. The contest played out as Grim tried to reach them. The Dark Lord reached forwards, but his blade was too high, and it was easy for the knight to get down on one knee and sink the crystal sword point-first into the Dark Lord's midriff.

Only then did Grim get Dog within range, his brother connecting with the knight's helmet in a brutal backhand swipe that sent him crashing to the floor.

The Dark Lord clutched at the crystal blade and sank to his knees. He looked up at Og-Grim-Dog.

And then he laughed.

'A clever trick, don't you think?' he said between chuckles.

'What do you mean?' asked Grim.

'There is no bane,' he said, sliding the crystal out of his body with a gasp of pain. 'Just a ruse to distract them from their real task. It worked quite well, no?'

Grim had to admit it had worked, though he couldn't help feeling that he and his brothers had been deceived, too.

'I hope you will forgive me,' said the Dark Lord, perhaps sensing the feelings of his henchman. 'But for such a ruse to work, everyone has to believe it. Not even Lilith knew. Now, I do hope Brother Kane survived the confrontation. Even though it's no bane, this weapon does leave a bit of a sting.'

*

Brother Kane's ministrations worked wonders. Even Gurin, whose injury would normally have taken his life, was set fair to make a full recovery within a few days. Grim was sure that Og's spear wound would have left him with a permanent disability without the cleric's attentions. Assata was back on her feet with no harm done and Simba was told to rest until his concussion had worn off.

All of which meant that the attack from the Bureau's adventurers, which had seemed so dangerous, had only cost the lives of around a hundred menials. Despite the Dark Lord's outward show of grief over these losses, no-one seriously thought it amounted to much of a loss. While the henchmen had dealt with the intruders upstairs, Lilith had won her battle with the enchantress and her charmed menials—the woman was dead by the time Grim had staggered down the stairs to investigate the scene.

In the end, however, the attack from the Bureau resulted in one more loss from Fell Towers. Assata called a meeting of her old friends. Brother Kane insisted it be held in Gurin's chamber, since the dwarf was not allowed to leave his bed yet.

'I'm leaving,' said the barbarian in her direct way. 'I was going to go anyway, after the wedding, but I can't stay here now. Do none of you feel even a shred of dishonour at slaughtering adventurers from Mer Khazer? It wasn't long ago that they were your colleagues, after all. It could have been any one of us who had come here.'

Grim really wasn't sure what he thought anymore. He knew that one of his brothers felt the same way as Assata and that the other didn't. He was caught in the middle, as ever.

'Oh, spare us the shame game,' Gurin retorted, propped up in his bed. 'You know very well that the Bureau has driven the likes of me and Og-Grim-Dog out. Where were these 'colleagues' of ours when we needed their support? What did they expect might become of us?'

'None of which makes what you are doing right. I know I regret my own actions.' Assata turned to Brother Kane with a dark look. 'And all the time you were a member of our dungeoneering party, you were secretly serving someone else. You would have betrayed every one of us if you'd been ordered to.'

Brother Kane gave Assata a beatific smile. 'Accept a blessing—' he began, fumbling for his vial of holy water.

Assata slapped at his hands. 'Spare me that fake act. You saved my life in Deepwood Dungeon. Were it not for that debt, I would be sorely tempted to strike you down right now. But this warning goes for all of you. By serving the Dark Lord you're willing to kill any of your former friends if ordered to do so. Know this. If we find ourselves on opposite sides in the future, I will be just as ready to do the same to you.'

With that, Assata left Fell Towers. Og held his tongue and stayed, though Grim knew he would have chosen to go with her.

A part of Grim felt the same way. But Assata had the Bureau and the Resistance. She belonged elsewhere. Og-Grim-Dog didn't belong anywhere but here.

A FACE IN THE FLAMES

Everyone at Fell Towers was now counting down the days to the wedding. The Dark Lord had a spring in his step. Princess Borte seemed increasingly quiet, perhaps resigned to her fate. Grim knew that she didn't want to be the wife of the Dark Lord. But he thought getting the wedding over with might actually do her good. She'd leave her cell in the basement behind, and become the Dark Lady.

Gurin's prolonged convalescence meant that Og-Grim-Dog had taken on some of the dwarf's duties as head of security. They frequently patrolled the walls of Fell Towers, keeping an eye on things. The attempt by the Bureau to stop the wedding had failed, but there was still the possibility that agents of the Kuthenian Empire might attempt to rescue the princess. And, the truth was, they had little faith in the menials to defend the stronghold without some help.

It was on one of their rounds, about the time afternoon turned into evening, that Dog caught sight of two figures leaving the stronghold via the postern gate.

'That's not the Dark Lord,' he commented, pointing down.

Indeed, they were used to seeing the Dark Lord using the gate for his cliffside walks. But not anyone else. From their vantage point, it wasn't hard to tell who it was. The first, even though she wore a drab looking cloak with the hood up, had the unmistakeable shapely figure of a woman; the other, long white hair that caught in the breeze.

'Mistress Lilith and Simba,' Og confirmed. 'I wonder where they are off to at this time?'

'And why they didn't mention they were going somewhere,' Grim added.

'They might have told Gurin,' Dog suggested, unwilling to cast aspersions. Nothing had been said, as such, but even Dog must have picked up on Og's disaffection with Fell Towers, and Grim's ambivalence.

'I think Gurin would have said something,' said Og. 'I am more than a little curious about what they are up to.'

An idea came to Grim. 'What about Raya's amulet?' he suggested.

Their friend, Raya the elf, had given them her magic amulet when they had been investigating the attack on the village of Urlay. An Amulet of Hiding, it made its wearer both invisible and silent. Very useful to a three-headed ogre who didn't want to draw attention to themselves.

'I don't know if we should be spying on them,' said Dog. 'It feels a bit disloyal.'

'Disloyal to whom?' asked Og slyly. 'Maybe the Dark Lord ought to know what they're up to?'

'I don't see the harm,' added Grim. 'After all, we can't be seen or heard, can we?'

'Alright then,' said Dog, knowing he was outvoted.

Og-Grim-Dog descended from the battlements to the rear of Fell Towers. Two menials were on guard at the postern gate.

'They've only just left,' one offered as they opened the gate for them.

'Good,' Grim said. 'Hopefully we'll catch them.'

Their task was made easier since the cliff walk was the only path available in this area. Everywhere else was steep, treacherous looking rock—the terrain giving Fell Towers its defensive strength as much as its walls and battlements. The salty tang of the sea air filled Grim's nostrils as he passed the spot where they had first met the Dark Lord. Once they were far enough away from the stronghold that prying eyes could no longer see them, Dog put on Raya's amulet. It was an odd kind of magic, because nothing changed as far as Grim could tell. He could see and hear his feet clomping along the path just the same; could see Og's pike swinging on the left and could hear Dog's stomach rumbling on the right. And yet, when they had worn the amulet in Mer Khazer and on their journey back from Urlay, they had been entirely invisible and silent to everyone else. They had to assume that the object still worked, since they knew nothing of magic.

After a long walk, the cliff path began taking them down to the beach, while to their right it opened onto a barren land of rocky bumps and dips. It made their task more difficult, since there were now more places that Lilith and Simba could have gone, and they had still seen no sign of them. Grim was beginning to think they simply weren't going to find them.

'Up there,' said Dog, pointing to a nearby hill.

Grim could just make out a faint flickering of light on the crest of the rocky mound. He shrugged. 'There's no other sign of life around here, and even if that's not them, it might afford us a view of the area.'

He headed for the hill, the ground steadily rising. The sun was beginning to set now and there was orange and pink in the sky as Grim began his ascent. He was breathing heavily by the time he approached the hilltop. He made no attempt to quieten his approach, trusting in the device around his brother's neck.

Suddenly, Simba was above them, looking down the hill. His eyes scanned past Og-Grim-Dog, looking in their direction, but not seeing them.

'Hello Simba,' Dog called up.

Grim gave his brother a stern look.

'What? I was just testing that the amulet worked.'

'Well be careful,' Og reprimanded. 'Dark elves have strange powers. I wouldn't be surprised if he sensed our approach, even if he can't see or hear us.'

'Then there is Mistress Lilith,' added Grim. 'She has powers, too.'

'What powers?' Dog asked, much quieter now.

'I'm not sure. There's something about her, though. Something more than human. And don't forget she defeated the enchantress during the attack on Fell Towers. She has magic, I'm telling you.'

Above them, Simba seemed to have satisfied himself that there were no intruders and retreated from the edge of the hilltop, allowing Grim to take the last few strides to the top. It was unusually flat and in its centre was a circle of half a dozen standing stones. Inside the circle was Lilith. She stood by a fire and Grim could hear her speaking into it. Its flames flickered with strange colours: blues and greens were mixed in with the oranges and yellows, and in the gathering darkness, it cast an eerie light.

'We need to get closer,' Og whispered.

Grim could see Simba patrolling on the opposite side of the stones. Gathering himself, he moved into the stone circle, only stopping when he was behind and slightly to the side of Lilith. From this position, all three brothers could look into the flames of the fire. All three could see the face that rippled in the flames, of the man that Lilith spoke with.

A handsome, human face looked out from the fire, though Grim couldn't help but notice that he had the same dark eyes as Lilith.

'Barclay has failed us, then,' the man said.

Barclay, Grim thought to himself. *There's a name I have heard before, though I can't recall where.*

'Maybe,' said Lilith. 'But he wasn't to know about the Dark Lord's ruse with the sword of Samir Durg. For all his idiocy, Jonty has a certain base cunning about him. I'm still uncertain about the depth of his powers and daren't challenge him alone. We are so close, now, but I still fear a setback if we get careless.'

'You worry too much, Lilith. Anyway, the Bureau was just one of our plans. Even if it would have been the simpler option, we still have our main hand to play.'

The Bureau? That's it, Grim told himself. *Barclay is the Director of the Bureau of Dungeoneering, the man who had ensured they were exiled from Mer Khazer. What was his connection to Lilith and this man in the flames? It sounded like they were all allies in some secret plot.*

'You must arrive here in three days' time, Samael,' said Lilith. 'No sooner or later. That is the day of the wedding and everyone will be distracted by the festivities, the Dark Lord most of all. I will ensure that the resistance here is minimal.'

'The Kuthenians are weak creatures,' the man Lilith had named Samael said with a sneer. 'But I will get them to Fell Towers in time, have no doubt. Three days and it is done.'

Grim began to back away from Lilith and her fire. He had heard enough, and if her unnatural conversation ended, he feared she might become more aware of her surroundings—might sense their presence. He already had suspicions that she was a magic user, but now it appeared that she was more powerful than he had imagined.

He left the stone circle behind, reached the edge of the hilltop and began the descent, moving as quickly as he dared.

'Well, that was interesting,' said Og with ironic understatement. 'Lilith a traitor? Kuthenians coming to Fell Towers? Even the Bureau is involved.'

'I have to admit,' said Dog, 'it was worth a visit. It seems like Simba is loyal to Mistress Lilith rather than the Dark Lord, too.'

'The question is,' said Grim, navigating his way down the hillside, 'what do we do about it?'

WEDDING CRASHERS

The next day, in the privacy of their room in the basement of Fell Towers, Og-Grim-Dog went back and forth over their options.

'There's no doubt in my mind,' said Grim, 'that Lilith intends to remove, almost certainly kill, the Dark Lord. She and her friend Samael made that clear enough. Why exactly, we can be less sure. What we also don't know is what that all means for us.'

'I believe,' said Og, 'this all boils down to our objectives here. Are we loyal followers of the Dark Lord? Or are we just in it for our food and lodging? In which case, what's to stop us siding with Lilith, if it looks like she's going to be on the winning side?'

A silence fell.

'Dog?' Grim pressed.

'What?'

'Come on now,' said Og. 'It's time to be honest with each other. You've been the one most in favour of our place here. To keep our place, we've had to do things I regret. We've murdered and kidnapped: hurt people we had no personal quarrel with. We've lost our friend Assata over it. What have we become? Unthinking beasts? Dogs that do their master's bidding in exchange for the scraps from his table?'

Dog snarled at that.

'I'm sorry,' said Og. 'That was a poor choice of words.'

Dog took a breath. 'No. You are right. I *am* just a mean dog, who only cares about where his next meal is coming from. But I know you are more than that, Og. I am sorry. This has gone far enough now. I've no loyalty to the Dark Lord or to Lilith. Both captivated me for a while, I'll admit. I thought I'd found somewhere to belong. We don't belong here. But if you're asking me what we should do now, I haven't got a clue.'

'You're not just a mean dog,' Og told him. 'We're all better than what we've become. But we still have some decisions to make. Do we warn the Dark Lord? Do we just escape alone in the night? Do we leave Princess Borte in her cell, or do we take moral responsibility for our part in putting her there?'

That was a lot to think about, and Grim felt as unable to fully answer Og's questions as his brothers. But he could see a first step, at least.

'I think we should tell Gurin what we know,' he said.

*

'I don't give two craps about the Dark Lord,' Gurin admitted once Og-Grim-Dog had filled him in on what they had observed. 'It's what you learned about the Bureau that interests me. Director Barclay,' he said the name with obvious distaste, 'the man behind the debasement of the adventuring life, is actually working for Lilith. Do you understand? The Bureau has been corrupted, its members sent here to eliminate the Dark Lord on *her* orders.'

Grim nodded. With all the revelations they had learned, he hadn't quite pieced together what it told them about the Bureau.

'I don't think it's just the Bureau, either.'

'What do you mean, Og?' Grim asked.

'Do you recall when we went dungeoneering in Wight's Hollow?' Og asked them.

'That disgrace of a place?' asked Gurin. 'Why are you reminding us of that?'

'There was a branch of Discount Dungeon Supplies there. I remember Assata suggesting that they were corrupting that place, in a fashion. Changing it into a tourist destination: not a real dungeon at all. Ever since, I've noticed how many branches of DDS there are around Gal'azu. When we returned here from Kuthenia, a DDS warehouse had appeared. It's replaced the Dark Lord's own weapons manufactory. A strange decision, if you ask me—making him dependent on others to keep his army supplied. And who was behind it?'

'Lilith,' Grim answered his brother. 'So she and this Samael she spoke to, what if they control DDS and the Bureau? It seems that Samael now has a measure of control over the Kuthenians, too, since he is leading an army this way. And now Lilith wants to remove the Dark Lord—'

'—and take over Fell Towers,' Dog finished for him.

'By The Maker's Mighty Beard,' said Gurin. 'There'll be no institution left in Gal'azu that they don't control. A hidden nexus controlling all the weapons and armies in the land—even the heroes who might have stood up to them.'

'And the food,' Og added.

'Eh? What do you mean?' Gurin demanded.

'Sheev's,' Og said simply.

'No!' said Dog. 'Don't tell me that Sheev's is now the enemy. This is going too far.'

'And for all we are learning,' said Grim, 'we still have to decide what we are going to do about it.'

'And quickly,' said Og. 'Because a Kuthenian army will be here in two days' time.'

✻

It was the night before the day before the wedding. Og-Grim-Dog was in the basement room they had begun to call home, though recent events meant they no longer used that word. Still, some things hadn't changed. Their job, as it had been for the last few weeks, was to keep an eye on the princess of the Kuthenian Empire. If anything, they were taking that duty more seriously than ever.

They took turns staying awake through the night while the other two slept. So it was, that when an unusual noise of clanking metal came from the basement—a noise which Grim would probably have slept through on previous nights—he woke his brothers and got to his feet.

Og-Grim-Dog took the time to light a lantern and then exited their room. The basement was especially dark at night-time, and as Og held the light in front of them, Grim was able to navigate towards Borte's cell.

As he neared, he saw a pale blue light that looked like it was hovering in the air, at about the same height as Og's lantern.

It wasn't until the bars of the prison cell came into view that he realised the light was held in the palm of a human wizard. It bathed Borte's cell in a gentle light, revealing an open door. Inside, a halfling was in the process of leading the princess out of her prison. They stopped, caught in the act, when they saw Grim approach. Movement next to the wizard caught his eye next, and an elf appeared at the mage's side. The bow she held was drawn and aimed their way. Finally, a voice from the darkness made him turn in the opposite direction to the prison cell. Here, Og's light identified a sword-wielding barbarian.

'We don't want to turn on you, Og-Grim-Dog,' said the voice. 'But if you try to intervene, we won't hesitate.'

The barbarian frowned slightly at the response.

Three ogre smiles appeared.

'Praise be to Lord Vyana and His Horde of Winged Hyenas,' said Dog. 'We're glad you're here.'

THE YELLOW WEDDING

The wedding breakfast was held in the Old Refectory. Tables full of menials occupied most of the space, while other menials acted as servers. They had already begun to circulate with the food, and the smell of fried bacon and hot syrup hung temptingly in the air.

No-one from Princess Borte's family was at the top table. Indeed, Princess Borte was not there herself, since in this part of Gal'azu it was considered bad luck for the groom to see the bride before the ceremony. Instead, joining the Dark Lord and Lilith, was the groom's mother, and various aunts, uncles and cousins.

Not far away was a table reserved for the Dark Lord's henchmen. Og-Grim-Dog sat on a bench next to Gurin. Opposite them were Simba and Brother Kane. Underneath the table was an invisible wizard by the name of Sandon Branderson. It had been agreed that Sandon would wear Raya's amulet and stay with Og-Grim-Dog and Gurin, in case they needed his help. It was only at the last minute that Raya had foreseen a problem with this part of the plan. Sandon was both invisible and silent, and would therefore struggle to communicate with them. To solve this problem, he had a parchment and quill with him, and would pass any messages he had on to Gurin.

The first of these was very unwelcome.

Grim could hear the dwarf whispering to Og. Leaving it a while, to avoid suspicion, Og quietly passed on the message to him.

'Don't eat the food.'

Sound advice, Grim supposed. The food was supplied by Sheev's, which if their suspicions were correct, was controlled by Lilith. They had overheard her assuring Samael that the resistance in Fell Towers today would be 'limited'. What better way to weaken the Dark Lord's soldiers than poison them at this breakfast?

Nonetheless, Grim gave a deep sigh. Asking Dog not to partake wasn't going to be easy.

As for Raya herself, she, Princess Borte, Assata and Hassletoff were long gone. They had left not long after Og-Grim-Dog had stumbled upon their rescue operation. It was agreed that they needed to get as far away from Fell Towers as possible before Borte's absence was discovered. It wasn't just the danger of the Dark Lord and his forces tracking them down. The Kuthenian army, with Lilith's ally Samael in tow, were due to arrive at Fell Towers too—and from everything Og-Grim-Dog had overheard, it was not a rescue force. They had come to take over Fell Towers, and their plans for Princess Borte were unlikely to be benign.

The servers arrived at their table with trays of pancakes, bacon and egg muffins, and bagels, with hot coffee and tea. As the feast was laid out, Grim took the opportunity to pass the warning on to his brother.

To his credit, Dog was able to control himself. He said nothing, instead gripping the edge of the table with his hand, until the fingers began to go white.

'These pancakes smell delicious,' said Simba. 'Here you go, Og-Grim-Dog,' he added, shoving the platter in their direction.

'Actually,' Grim responded through clenched teeth, 'we ate rather a large supper last night. Silly, really, but none of us has much of an appetite this morning. Please, don't let us stop you enjoying it, though. Those muffins look very tempting.'

Simba gave the muffins a nervous look. 'I would,' he replied, 'but I'm actually trying to cut wheat out of my diet.'

'You could always scoff out the bacon and eggs,' Og suggested. 'No-one here will mind, I'm sure.'

'Can I pour the drinks?' asked Brother Kane, who was due to lead the service later that day. 'Even if you're not hungry, I'm sure you can manage a nice cuppa.'

'What a shame,' said Gurin, looking suspiciously at the pots, steam visibly rising from the spouts. 'I've recently decided to go caffeine free.'

This awkward charade was interrupted by the arrival of the Dark Lord at the table, accompanied by his mother. She had taken the trouble to put on a nice dress for the wedding and Grim thought she had a kind face. However, he could see her eyes widen in horror at the sight of some of her son's associates. She seemed to like the look of Brother Kane, however, and after her son introduced everyone, she stood next to him, one hand on his shoulder.

'It must be a very proud day,' Gurin offered into the silence.

'Yes,' she said, 'though I do wish with all my heart that Jonty's brother, Fraser, was here. Such a sweet boy, he was. It's the not knowing where he is that hurts the most.'

'Oh, mum,' said the Dark Lord irritably. 'Knowing Fraser, he's probably partying in some dive somewhere, perfectly safe, with not a thought for the rest of us.'

'Yes,' Og agreed. 'He's probably a lot closer than you think.'

The Dark Lord's helmeted head turned towards Og, and it was easy to imagine there was a withering look on his face. He soon led his mother away, and the henchmen returned their attention to the trays of food and drink on the table, now going cold.

Dog's hand, still gripping the edge of the table, now began to shake, as he tried to resist every natural compulsion he had.

Lilith appeared, and now she too glared at the food on the table. 'No-one's eating?' she asked, a dangerous edge to her voice.

'Apparently,' Simba said, 'Og-Grim-Dog are too full.'

Lilith turned her dark-eyed gaze to Og-Grim-Dog. 'I find that almost impossible to believe,' she said. Unable to look away, Grim found her gaze holding him, searching his thoughts for evidence of treachery. He tried to keep his mind blank—tried to stop it revealing what he knew. But the more he struggled, the more those memories threatened to enter his consciousness. It was only at this moment that Grim got a true sense of the woman's power, and it was terrifying.

'On second thoughts,' said Dog, his hand coming away from the table's edge, 'I am getting a little bit peckish.'

He reached for a muffin. Everybody watched, as slowly, he brought the food to his mouth, and let it drop in. Everybody continued to watch, in absorbed silence, as he chewed and swallowed. 'Mmm,' Dog said appreciatively. 'Very nice.'

Lilith relaxed then, and she allowed a satisfied little smile to appear on her face. 'Good. I am pleased,' she said, and returned to her place at the top table.

Dog belched loudly.

'That doesn't smell too good,' said Grim, wishing he had a hand to waft away the smell, or to hold his nose.

'I'm not sure I feel too good,' said Dog.

'No, well, you've probably just eaten a poisoned muffin.'

Come to think of it, Grim wasn't feeling too good, either. He wasn't sure what happened to the food that he and his brothers ate, but he had a suspicion that it all ended up in the same place.

'We may have a problem after eating that muffin,' Grim warned Og.

'Look around,' said Og. 'We won't be the only ones.'

Many of the menials seated at the tables were clutching their stomachs, or grumbling to one another. Any remaining doubts Grim had about Lilith's plan disappeared at the sight of the Dark Lord's forces withering before his eyes. And now was the moment Mistress Lilith chose to begin proceedings.

She rapped on the table for quiet. 'It is time to fetch the new Lady of Fell Towers,' she announced in a voice that carried around the room. Her words were met by a mixture of polite applause and wind, the latter of which, Grim feared, was emanating from both orifices. 'Og-Grim-Dog, you have the honour.'

Grim got to his feet and proceeded to leave the Refectory at what he hoped was a stately pace. He felt his stomach roil in protest as he left the Refectory and headed for the trapdoor to the basement.

'At least we had just the one muffin,' he muttered under his breath.

'We'll be fine,' said Og. 'Though I'm not so sure about those menials in the Refectory, who must have ingested much more poison than Dog.'

Grim had to agree. The menials also lacked the fearsome digestive tract of an ogre, which was capable of dealing with virtually anything its owner sent there.

The two menials on guard duty were already raising the trapdoor at Og-Grim-Dog's approach.

'It's exciting, isn't it?' one of them suggested.

'You don't know the half of it,' said Dog. 'I recommend you stand back a little,' he said cryptically, as Grim began to descend the stairs to the basement.

He got a shock when Sandon suddenly appeared next to them, the amulet in one hand.

'Lord Vyana's whiskers, Sandon!' Dog let out. 'I nearly flattened you with my mace!'

'Apologies, Dog,' said Sandon. 'I just thought I ought to let you know. The Dark Lord's adviser—'

'Mistress Lilith?'

'Yes. I snuck a look at her when she came over to the table. I'm afraid to say, I believe she's a succubus.'

No doubt Grim should have known what a succubus was, but he didn't.

'A suck you what?' demanded Dog.

'A demon. A very powerful demon. Whatever happens now, please be aware that she possesses far more power than I do—perhaps more power than any other creature in Gal'azu. Under no circumstances do we take her on. As soon as we get the chance, we need to get out of here.'

'Well,' said Grim, 'here's our chance. Fraser?' he called into the darkness of the basement.

Grim detected a slither of movement at the bottom of the steps.

'Back up a little,' came Fraser's voice. 'She's hungry.'

Grim and Sandon retreated up the steps. 'I said get back!' Dog ordered the two menials as they cleared a space around the trapdoor.

They all fixed their attention on the exit to the basement, as a giant worm's head appeared at the top of the steps. As it slithered its way into the hall, its rider was revealed—Fraser, the imprisoned older brother of the Dark Lord—imprisoned no longer. He blinked in the light, his gaunt frame looking almost skeletal in contrast to Evie, the Dark Lord's plump, fleshy pet.

Fraser flashed them a vicious grin. 'I've been waiting for this moment,' he stated. 'Forward, Evie!' he cried, and the worm responded, heading for the sounds and smells of the Old Refectory.

'What are we going to do?' asked one of the menials.

'We're going to watch,' said Dog, and, taking the hint, Grim followed in Evie's wake. Sandon had disappeared once more, but Grim assumed the wizard wasn't far away.

A predictable chorus of shouts and screams erupted from the wedding reception, and Grim re-entered the room to see Fraser guiding Evie towards the top table. A few loyal menials staggered over to bar their path, but the worm sucked them up into its maw and few chose to intervene after that, complaining to each other about their upset stomachs.

'Hello, brother!' Fraser crowed with delight, as he bore down on the Dark Lord. 'Your pet monster has already eaten your bride to be. Now it's your turn!'

Good, Grim said to himself. Part of the deal they had struck with Fraser was that he would announce Princess Borte's death. It made it less likely she would be hunted.

Lilith quickly evacuated the top table, staring at the giant worm with an intense fascination.

'Destroy them!' the Dark Lord demanded, but she shook her head.

'Down Evie!' the Dark Lord instructed, but his pet let out a high-pitched whistling noise, that suggested it was not going to oblige.

He raised his hands, as if to cast some spell of protection. But no magic appeared, and the Dark Lord's helmeted head swivelled around to look at Lilith. A smirk of pleasure met him, as the succubus' own powers countered his.

'Is that you, Fraser?' asked the Dark Lord's mother, looking up as Evie opened its maw and began to rise into the air.

'Yes, it's me! Finally free, after years locked up in Jonty's dungeon!'

'Is that true, Jonty?'

'Henchmen!' the Dark Lord called out, ignoring his mother. 'Deal with this beast!'

Simba was already at his true master's side, watching on impassively next to Mistress Lilith.

Gurin shrugged. 'I don't think so.'

'Brother Kane!?' the Dark Lord pleaded.

'My son is not about to help you,' exclaimed Lilith, her face lighting up in a cruel smile as the worm reared higher.

'Her son?' Dog said. 'How old is she?'

'You did pick up on the fact that she's a demon?' Grim asked him.

'Yes. A very good looking one, though.'

Grim sighed. 'Never mind.'

The Dark Lord was looking at them now, his last hope. 'Ogre?' he asked. 'Is this your doing?'

He never learned our name, Grim noted.

Evie launched herself downwards and swallowed the Dark Lord whole. An unpleasant eating sound followed, before the worm spat out the Dark Lord's helmet. It landed on the floor with a metallic clang.

'Come on, mother,' said Fraser. 'Let's get out of here.'

He offered his hand. She seemed to consider it for a second, and then took Fraser's hand and clambered onto the worm until she was seated behind her older son, arms clinging around his waist.

'No-one had better try anything,' Fraser warned.

Lilith waved a hand, instructing her followers to let him go. After all, he had done her a favour. The Dark Lord was gone, and she hadn't had to do the deed, nor had Samael and his Kuthenian army had to lay siege to Fell Towers. She was in charge now.

Fraser turned Evie around and left the room the way they had come in, heading for the exit to the keep, and no doubt on to the gates to Fell Towers. Grim was pleased. The basement of Fell Towers was empty now, and he believed that was as it should be.

Grim felt himself pulled to the right, and saw that Dog's arm was being yanked by some invisible force. Sandon obviously wanted them out of there in a hurry. He made a face at Gurin, who started to head in their direction.

Fortunately, their movements were going unnoticed so far. Simba had collected the Dark Lord's helmet and was now holding it out for Lilith.

'Show your obedience to our new Dark Lord!' he bellowed into the room. With no small amount of grumbling and clutching of stomachs, the menials in the Refectory all got down on one knee.

Simba placed the horned helmet onto Lilith's head.

'Servants of the Dark Lord!' she said to the room, her voice supernaturally loud. 'Serve me as you served your former leader and you will be rewarded! Know that under my rule our evil empire will grow, as we form alliances with the Kuthenian Empire and the Dark Elves of Cly'ath Denori'Kilith Tu'an.'

Instead of a great cheer, this announcement was met with an uncertain silence. Into the silence, came the distinct sound of somebody hurling, followed by the splatter of vomit on the floor. Then, as if that one individual disgorgement acted as a trigger, a cascade of chunks surged up from the stomachs of many a menial—each emitted stream merging to form a sea of sickness that swept across the room. The sudden sour smell hit Grim like a slap in the face.

'Grim,' Dog moaned, please get us out of here.

Grim didn't need to be told twice, leaving at pace. Gurin was not far behind, unable to suppress an audible obscenity as he was forced to wade through the spill. Dog dry heaved once, but managed not to lose the contents of his stomach.

'The postern gate is this way,' Grim said to Gurin as the dwarf caught up to them.

The menials on guard duty saw them approach and opened the gate for them.

'Has the wedding been fun?' one of them asked.

'The Dark Lord was eaten by a worm,' Dog answered honestly.

'Oh.'

Once outside, Sandon appeared with them.

'What's that your carrying?' asked Og, gesturing at a staff the wizard held.

'I found it upstairs. It belonged to Relandra the Enchantress. She was a friend of mine. Are you sure this is the best way out?' he asked as Grim led them along the cliff walk.

'Samael and the Kuthenians will be coming up the road to the front gates of the stronghold,' Og answered, allowing Grim to concentrate on moving as fast as he could. 'We don't want to have to sneak past them. This is a longer route, but safer.'

'Very well,' said Sandon. 'Here, have the amulet back. You're the most conspicuous of us all, you might need it.'

Og grabbed the magic item from the wizard.

'Did you like my Spell of Regurgitation?' the wizard asked, just as the sea air had expunged the smell of the Refectory from Grim's nostrils.

'That was you?' asked Dog.

'Yes. I got the idea from my time in the city state of Rapoli. Do you know, the noble families of the city deliberately bring up the earlier courses of a meal, just so—'

'Please, Sandon,' said Gurin. 'Not now.'

'Oh, alright. Maybe I should tell you that story later.'

'There's one good thing about it, I suppose,' said Dog.

'What's that?'

'I don't think I'll miss the Dark Lord's Refectory so much after that.'

A SCORE TO SETTLE

It was a long and tiresome trek through the badlands that surrounded Fell Towers. At first, Og-Grim-Dog, Gurin and Sandon were nervous of being followed by the agents of the new Dark Lord. Once it became clear that they weren't, the boredom of walking all day soon set in. The time was taken up by Sandon's stories of all the places he had been, and Dog's stories of all the famous people he claimed to have met. It didn't take long for Grim to wish they *were* being chased.

But every journey has an end, and this one ended outside the opening to a dungeon, just north of the Moors of Misery. It was Wight's Hollow, a place they had agreed on with Assata, Raya and the others as a good location to meet, should they all make it out of Fell Towers. Here they were reunited with their friends. It looked like the exercise and fresh air had done Princess Borte good. She raised an eyebrow at their appearance but said nothing. Grim wondered what she really thought of these people, who had kidnapped her, taken her to be married against her will to a madman, and then released her at the last moment. Probably, that they were rather stupid.

Sat with her around a fire were Assata, Raya and Hassletoff. The halfling tended to a pot that, if Grim's nose wasn't mistaken, contained a meat broth.

'Fond memories of this place?' asked the barbarian sarcastically in greeting.

Wight's Hollow had been a low point of their dungeon crawl last year. It wasn't really a dungeon at all any longer—more of a shopping excursion.

'Knowing that Lilith and Samael control both the Bureau and Discount Dungeon Supplies means this place makes a lot more sense than it did,' Og replied.

Mention of their new enemies brought forth serious expressions on the faces of those who gathered about the fire.

'I'm sorry about Brother Kane,' said Raya. 'If I'd known he was working for the Dark Lord, I'd have warned you.'

The elf's apology surprised Grim. Did she really blame herself, or Brother Kane, for the things they had done? Grim knew they didn't deserve such an easy let off. Even so, it was a kind thought, and it made it a little easier to take his place by the fire with these people—people he felt he had let down in some way.

Over supper, they told the others what had happened at Fell Towers after they had left that night. Again, Princess Borte spoke little and didn't react very much when she heard of the death of the Dark Lord. They were unable to say for sure what became of Fraser in the end, but they all agreed that Evie gave him a good chance of completing his escape.

Sandon told them what he knew of succubae. Demons able to take the female form, they could tie lesser beings to their will. The more they discussed Sheev's, Discount Dungeon Supplies and the Kuthenian Empire, the more they realised what a devilish plot Lilith had constructed.

Then, finally, perhaps the strangest revelation of all. 'Brother Kane, it turns out, is this creature's son,' said Sandon.

'Sired by whom?' Hassletoff asked.

'That, we don't know,' said Sandon. 'Kane is not a wizard, but he has formidable powers. We can speculate that he derives them, at least in part, from his demon heritage.'

'When we got sight of the Kuthenian army heading for Fell Towers, I left Raya, Toff and Borte for a while,' Assata explained next. 'It wasn't that hard for me to infiltrate their camp, disguised as a slave,' she said, a touch of bitterness to her voice. 'I learned that the new emperor is Tugh. Princess Borte's uncle.'

'I believe that solves the riddle of who killed my father,' said the princess. She controlled her emotions, but it was not hard to see her pain. 'Samael was a trusted official at my father's court. No doubt in the confusion caused by my abduction, it was easy for Samael and my uncle to blame the assassination on the agents of the Dark Lord. I don't doubt that was a part of Lilith and Samael's plan all along. My uncle will be a more malleable ruler for Samael to control than my father was.'

'Tugh appointed a general of the army,' Assata continued, 'ostensibly with orders to rescue Borte and punish the Dark Lord. But it was obvious that Samael had the real control.'

'And I'm almost certain,' Sandon added, 'that this Samael is an incubus. The male version of a succubus. He and Lilith have been working together to win control over Pengshui and Fell Towers for some time. Now they have it. And I fear for Gal'azu. It's not just that they now control the two largest armies in the land. Even though we have discovered their true natures, I know of no-one and nothing with the power to destroy them.'

And we helped to eliminate any heroes who might have been able to challenge them, Grim realised. He would keep that fact to himself. His friends might have forgiven Og-Grim-Dog for their other crimes, but if they knew what they had done in Varena...

'Sounds like we'll have to wait until we can deal with that pair,' Gurin agreed. 'But I think there is one score we can settle right now.'

❋

All seven of them trekked through the Moors of Misery for the south. For Mer Khazer. Grim had an odd feeling that they were returning home, even though they had spent so little time in the town. But, he supposed, some places are just like that.

Borte, relieved to discover that not all of western Gal'azu was badlands or unending moors, took pleasure in the raw beauty of this part of the world. More than once, Grim noticed the princess and Assata talking quietly together, comparing the way of life here with Kuthenia. At some point, he didn't know when, their mutual animosity had faded away and now their relationship appeared quite different. Someone had armed Borte with a short spear. Grim had no idea if she knew how to use it, but it seemed that as each day passed, she was becoming more an adventurer, and less a princess.

In this company, Og and Dog didn't have to hide their heads in sacks, nor did they have to use Raya's amulet. If the human travellers on the roads didn't like the look of a three-headed ogre travelling with such an unusual collection of individuals, they were at least wise enough to keep their opinions to themselves. Raya herself, meanwhile, scouted ahead and all around, in case more hostile eyes watched them. But orcs and goblins tended not to interfere with ogres, and trolls rarely gathered in numbers large enough for them to challenge a group such as theirs. So it was that their destination appeared on the horizon at the end of a trouble-free journey.

'We're banned from Mer Khazer,' Og reminded everyone. 'They won't let us in.'

'I had to give up my position as reeve to go adventuring to Fell Towers,' Hassletoff explained as they reached the town gates. 'I just have to hope that there's a friendly face on duty today.'

THE DIRECTOR

I really shouldn't be letting you in,' said the young man, in a tone that suggested he was already half inclined to do just that.

'We've important business to deal with, Oliver,' Hassletoff said. 'I wouldn't ask you to bend the rules otherwise. Would I?'

Oliver answered the question by waving them all through into the town. The halfling patted the young man on the back. 'You've done the right thing.'

'We don't want to waste time or alert Barclay to our arrival,' said Gurin as they marched down the main street towards the centre of town. 'Where's he likely to be? The Bureau?'

'No,' said Hassletoff. 'His townhouse. It's well guarded. And let's not forget that Barclay is a powerful sorcerer. We'll need some sort of plan to deal with him.'

Grim had to admit, it felt good to be preparing for battle. Their time at Fell Towers had ended in retreat, and he felt as if they had unfinished business. Bones that needed to be broken; blood that needed to be spilled.

'I think they've had enough time,' Gurin murmured next to him, 'for it to have worked, or not.'

They had decided to send Hassletoff and Sandon into the house ahead of them, on the pretext of needing to talk with Barclay about what they had found at Fell Towers. They assumed that he would be eager to hear news of how things went with his secret allies. The

132

danger: that he already knew and was able, through his magic, to communicate with Lilith and Samael.

'Agreed,' said Assata on Grim's other side.

'Agreed,' said Og and Dog.

Grim stepped out of their hidden position and began marching towards the front door of Barclay's house, where two heavily armoured warriors stood on watch. Gurin and Assata followed behind and the warriors were already shouting out a warning.

Grim picked up the pace, as the door to the house swung open and more warriors surged out. Og hefted his pike and Dog let out a great bark of exultation. Barclay's elite warriors, their expensive armour polished to a shine, their weapons sharpened to a razor's edge, their heads encased in metal helms, showed no hesitation at the sight of an ogre coming for them. Instead they came to meet the threat, confident in their ability, shields ready to take the first blow from Og's pike.

Then the nearest of them went down, as a well-aimed missile whistled through the thin slit of his helmet, striking one of the few unprotected parts of his body.

The warrior next to him didn't let that put him off, and his shield met Og's strike, the weight of his armour helping him to absorb the blow. Then more blows could be heard, as Gurin wielded his axe, and Assata her sword.

Og's pike was now held out horizontally before them, and Grim was charging forwards, his powerful thighs and hips driving forwards, using his size to unsettle the enemy as the pike hit them at chest height.

Barclay's warriors didn't do so bad, one of them even cutting Og's pike in half, so that he was left holding a glorified stick. But Dog was in amongst them now. Plate mail can stop a lot of things, Grim mused. But not an ogre's mace. It came down on heads, shoulders and arms, metal crumpling and buckling and twisting—muscles tearing and bones snapping from the blunt force trauma. When he was done, a battered semi-circle of bodies was sprawled on the floor around him. Gurin and Assata tidied up any warriors still on their feet.

Some still lived, groaning in pain, one of them screaming—a horrible, high-pitched sound that pierced Grim's ears and rang in his head. But they were incapacitated, that was what mattered. Grim led his friends to the door of the house. From behind a tree, Raya emerged, bow already nocked with another arrow.

Inside, the Director's front room was laid out as a hall, with a fire and table dominating the space. Fresh rushes covered the floor and an expensive tapestry ran across one wall. At the far end of the room, Director Barclay had only one warrior left. Next to them were Sandon and Hassletoff.

Barclay wore a black robe and held a wooden staff. He gave a sardonic look as Og-Grim-Dog led his friends into the Director of the Bureau's house.

'I am beginning to see what this is,' he said. 'A revolution? Dwarves and ogres back in the Bureau?' He turned to look at Sandon and Hassletoff. 'Freeing the Bureau from the clandestine control of dark forces?'

He smiled as their reactions gave away the truth.

'You've betrayed the Bureau,' Sandon said.

He raised his new staff, the blue orb on the top emitting a magical light, but Barclay saw it coming. A flick of his staff and Sandon was sent to the floor, held in place by some vast, unseen force.

When Hassletoff reached for his hilt, Barclay's warrior did the same, and the halfling backed away instead.

Barclay sighed at the stupidity of his opponents. He looked back to Og-Grim-Dog and his friends, who were slowly approaching the sorcerer, as if playing a game of grandmother's footsteps. 'Even if you could kill *me*,' he said, 'Samael and Lilith would exact a terrible revenge. Is that what you want?'

'We'll deal with them when the time comes,' Gurin said.

Barclay twisted his face in derision. 'Don't be a child. The Bureau completely disbanded? The utter end of our way of life? These are the choices I have had to make, in the real world. It's easy to be an old romantic and complain that the world isn't perfect from the sidelines. I'm the best defence from those monsters that our community has. I don't expect gratitude—'

Director Barclay said no more, as from nowhere a short spear erupted from his throat, the metal blade rising upwards and stopping when it hit his chin.

His remaining guard spun around and drew his sword in one motion, but there was no adversary to be seen, and while he looked for one, Hassletoff was upon him, burying his own sword in his back. The guard's sword came for the halfling, but it was not hard for Hassletoff to duck under the blow and jump out of the way. By that point, Sandon was back on his feet and a blast of magic sent the mailed warrior to the floor.

It wasn't pleasant to watch Director Barclay's eyes bulge in surprise or hear his wet chokes. But after that, mercifully, he died quickly.

Behind his prone form, Princess Borte suddenly appeared, Raya's amulet in one hand.

Hassletoff retrieved his sword. 'So, we can expect a terrible revenge now?' he asked.

'There's one silver lining,' said Borte, her face pale and her voice a monotone as she looked at the man she had killed. 'My father and the Dark Lord didn't know what was coming for them. We do.'

＊

They didn't waste any time. The very next day, the adventurers of Mer Khazer agreed to make Hassletoff the new Director of the Bureau of Dungeoneering. One of his first acts was to amend the constitution and identify dwarves, elves and halflings as racial groups, with as much right to be members of the Bureau as humans.

Ogres? Well, he promised to set up a committee to investigate the status of other races. In the meantime, he made Og-Grim-Dog an honorary member of the Bureau.

Grim walked with Gurin to the gates of Mer Khazer. The dwarf carried a heavy pack on his shoulders. 'I don't really understand,' said Grim. 'You've only just won your place back in the Bureau and you're leaving?'

'Yes, well. I have something to set right first. But I will return.'

'Something to set right?' asked Og. 'You're talking about the evil act you committed for the Dark Lord, aren't you?'

The dwarf made a face. 'That obvious is it?'

'Oh, my Lord Vyana!' exclaimed Dog. 'You're going to tell us what it is, aren't you?'

Gurin sighed. 'Alright, but it goes no further. I mean it!'

'Of course,' Og-Grim-Dog agreed.

'It's to do with Hurin, Durin, Thurin, Kurin, Tony and Maurin.'

'I knew it!' said Grim. 'Wait, you didn't kill them?'

'Kill them? Of course not. I merely sold them to a travelling circus.'

'You sold them? Into slavery?'

'They're not slaves as such. They just have to work for the circus for no money and aren't allowed to leave. Anyway, that was my dark deed. I'm not proud of it. But I will do my best to make amends. And that has to count for something, right?'

A PARTING

In the Flayed Testicles, an eerie silence greeted the end of the Landlord's story. His customers had learned a lot more about his past, and not all of it had been good.

'So,' said the Recorder, as he shuffled his parchment into a neat pile. 'You had tried the life of a hero and a villain?'

'Yes,' said the middle head. 'And neither of them really worked out for us. Now don't get me wrong. I'm sure there's some people who are perfectly suited to such roles. Just not us.'

'Interesting,' said the Recorder in a cryptic manner. 'So, Gurin the dwarf revealed to you the price he paid for a position with the Dark Lord. Betraying his six closest compatriots. Meanwhile, you maintain that the Dark Lord required nothing from you?'

An ominous growl from the Landlord was the only response to the Recorder's interrogation.

'Fair enough,' the man conceded. He patted his pile of parchment. 'Now, I need to return to my Publishing House. There they will make the first copy of these stories, and that will be used to make all subsequent copies. It is a long and laborious process. All in all, it will be some time before I can return.'

'That's fine with us,' said the Landlord's third head. 'The next part of our life story won't be easy to tell. We will need some time to think about how best to do it.'

'Indeed,' said the Recorder, with some sympathy. 'Based on where you ended tonight, I can only assume that what followed was The War of The Dead.'

'That's right,' said the first head. 'And there were no heroes or villains in that war. Just those who survived somehow, and those who didn't.'

END CREDITS

Three pairs of ogre eyes watched from the doorway of The Testicles, as the Recorder rode out of town, on a pony just as dishevelled looking as its owner.

'He knows what we did,' said the middle head.

'He was just fishing,' the third head reassured. 'Our secret is safe.'

***

Thanks to my beta readers: Lisa Maughan, Lana Turner & Marcus Nilsson.

Thanks to everyone else who has supported my work.

CONNECT WITH THE AUTHOR

Subscribe to Jamie's newsletter to claim your free digital copy of the prequel to The Weapon Takers Saga, *Striking Out*

https://subscribe.jamieedmundson.com/

Website:

jamieedmundson.com

Twitter:

@jamie_edmundson

Og-Grim-Dog and The War of The Dead

The dead walk Gal'azu in the third novel of the Me Three series.

Lightning Source UK Ltd.
Milton Keynes UK
UKHW041307050123
414884UK00004B/305

9 781912 221073